Chasing Christmas

Only Love Could Be Better Than Freedom

Book Four and a Half in

The Fairies Saga

USA Today Bestselling Author

Dani Haviland

Early winter 1783, remote North Carolina: Rejuvenated time traveler Evie and her family have little in life but each other, but they're content. When her husband rescues an abused young Native American woman and brings her home, she's welcomed. Unexpected births, deaths, and a marriage change the dynamics of this unique family in this stand-alone novella featuring many of the characters from the popular time travel series *The Fairies Saga.*

1 Amateur Surgeon

Late spring 1783

Dinner was finished, my two-year-old triplets had all used the privy and were in bed, and now I was answering a different kind of call of nature: that of midwife to my adopted daughter Jenny's pet Angora goat. My husband Wallace had come out to help after he and Jenny finished with the after dinner and before bedtime routines of washing dishes and a bedtime story for the three little ones.

I had been in the barn with Sarah P, the partially pregnant goat, for at least two hours. The first kid came out without a problem. However, the second one was stuck inside her. I had been trying to maneuver it in utero, kneading and manipulating the nanny's belly to get the baby's head down so she or he could be born, but the pushing and urging did nothing. The kid was still crossways in the womb; I couldn't get either the head or feet pointed to the exit.

I huffed and grunted in frustration, but that didn't help either.

"Wallace, I have to do something for her! I can't stand to see her suffer. Good grief, if Sarah was here, she'd know how to do it."

"How to do what?" he asked, busy with a fistful of straw, wiping the birth fluids off the first kid—a pure white female—that I had just delivered.

Still seated on the milking stool now repurposed into a midwife's bench, I set my chin in my hands. "Perform a C-section," I said glumly.

"What's that?"

"It stands for Caesarian section. That's where the mother's belly is cut open and the baby is pulled out. Supposedly, that's how Julius Caesar was born. Anyway, it's quite common when I come from, but I haven't done anything even remotely like that before. Only qualified surgeons with anesthetics and antibiotics would even attempt it."

"But, you just said that Julius Caesar was born that way. They didn't have anas…anasteth…well, they didn't have what you're telling me you need. But, I'm sure they had sharp knives. That's pretty much the most important part, right?"

"Yeah, well, Caesar probably wasn't born that way, but I *know* they've been successfully delivering babies by C-

2

section for well over a hundred years, and all over the world, too. Hmph, I can't see how she'd be in any more pain if I cut the kid out of her than if I left it inside. If we—or I—don't do something soon, they'll both die."

I shifted position and turned toward the house. "Jenny," I hollered. "Oh, there you are. Honey, I need to do a medical procedure on Sarah P so would you get me the..."

Jenny brought her hand out from behind her back, revealing my chair-side sewing kit. "Can we help?"

I looked behind her and saw Scout holding up a bottle of whisky. He grinned and shrugged his shoulder but didn't say anything.

"What are you doing with that whisky?" Wallace asked, slightly indignant that the young visitor had helped himself to the family's liquor.

"Jenny said ye'd need it. I mean, she said Evie wanted it. And this, too." He brought out the paring knife from behind his back. "Ye did want them, dinna ye?" he asked uneasily.

Just then, Sarah P bleated in agony, sounding so much like a woman that it gave me the chills. "Yes, you two brought me everything I need. Now since you're both here, I'd like your help, too. Wallace, would you bind Bristol, that's the first kid, in a blanket and put her in the corner? I need you to hold one end of Sarah P. Scout and Jenny can hold the other end while I make the incision. On second thought, Wallace, you're stronger; you get the back legs."

Everyone grabbed a leg or two and I said a quick, "Lord, guide my hand and help me help her and the baby within; in Jesus name, Amen." I poured whisky over the blade of the paring knife and neared the nanny's bloated belly. "Shoot!" I said, glad that the expletive had changed into a verb on its way out. "I wish I could knock her out."

"Here, let me try," Wallace said. He released one of her legs, letting it pump air in pain and frustration, and used his free hand to place direct pressure on the side of her neck. She melted like an ice cube in summer, limp as cooked lettuce.

"Cool, the Spock grip," I said. "Let's get going. Keep hold of her legs, though, just in case she wakes up."

"Spock grip?" Wallace asked. "I think it's the carotid artery I put pressure on so the oxygen to her brain was depleted, causing her to lose consciousness. Oops, sorry; you need to concentrate."

I glanced at him and gave a combination grin and

grimace, and then bent to my work. The first cut bled a lot but didn't get down to the uterine wall. Jenny took a rag and wordlessly, without prompting, wiped the blood from the cut. "I have to cut deeper," I said to myself as much as to them. They all watched intently, concentrating on what I was doing, as if it would help me perform my task. Actually, I think it did help. At least, I wasn't distracted.

Another firm cut and I was in. I turned away as the water from the second birth sac squirted in my face, then wiped it away with my shoulder. I quickly set the knife down and pulled out the second kid—this one male—and handed him to Scout. "Here, hold him while I sew her back up. Wallace, get ready to zap her carotid if she starts moving again."

Jenny handed me a threaded needle, anticipating my need before I even asked for it. Well, at least she lets me *think* it first. "Thanks," I said, then bent to the task: cross stitching on a nanny goat's belly.

***

Jody and his wife Sarah, my mother-in-law and the most popular healer in our part of the state, came back the next afternoon. "I'm impressed," Sarah said after checking on my patient.

I shrugged my shoulder in modesty, then smirked and asked, "Impressed with the job I did or that I even did it at all?"

"I'm impressed with the job. You always seem to come through, ready and willing to perform whatever task needs done, whether you think you're capable of it or not. Or whether you believe you have the correct tools or environment. But, the stitching is nice, too. It's a good thing she's young. She'll heal quickly, I'm sure. I'm curious though, where'd you dig up such odd names for the kids: Bristol and Track?"

"I don't know; they just popped into my head. They must mean something, though, because Leah howled when I told her the names. James didn't know what was so funny, so I think it's something from my past life. If it's that hilarious, it's probably something embarrassing, and I don't want to know about it. Nevertheless, the names just sounded right for the first two offspring of Sarah P and Todd. Leah said I used to know them; a married couple named Sarah and Todd but didn't say any more about them. Either way, the goats will both produce beautiful, soft fleece, and we can shear them twice as often as sheep. I guess they must be Scotch angoras—mighty thrifty critters."

***

A few days later, Scout's father—who also happened to be my ex-husband and the sperm donor to my triplets—showed up with a satchel filled to the brim with hostility and nothing else. "Let's go," he said to Scout. "Gather yer belongings. Ye've bothered these folks long enough."

"He's no bother," I said, waiting for the glare of anger that had fueled our rift three years earlier.

And there it was. Brown eyes narrowed, jaw thrust forward, nostrils flared. There was no doubt in my mind that he was holding back words and actions that nearly gagged him. He swallowed hard to compose himself then counted to five under his breath. "He's my son and my responsibility. We have many miles to travel, so I'd *appreciate it* if he gathered what is his and came along."

Wallace had been plowing in what we called the south forty and had seen Ian come to the house. He shimmied out from under the harness he wore to turn the soil—we had no mule—and sprinted to the edge of the yard, walking the last bit to catch his breath. "Good day to you, Ian," he said with what I knew to be feigned courtesy. When Ian showed up, discomfort was sure to be close behind.

"Good day to you, too, cousin," he said. "I've come to take with me what is mine. Wee Ian is in need of education; one better than counting, reading, and shucking corn."

Wallace's eyes opened wide in shock at the insult, then narrowed in disgust. *"Scout,"* he said, stressing the name that all of us, including the boy, preferred, "is old enough to make up his own mind about where he'd like to get his *education.*"

"I'm his father, and I'll decide where he goes and what he learns," Ian growled, his face red with barely contained rage, his bulging eyes positively scary.

Wallace took two steps closer to Ian. He was a full five inches taller than his cousin, and although he wasn't a violent man, he wasn't above intimidation.

"Yer height doesna bother me. Now, where is he?"

"I'm right here. I was just gatherin' a few items to take with me and sayin' good-bye to Jenny." He turned and looked back at Jenny, her cheeks wet with tears, her eyes red and swollen. "Ye ken I'll be back soon, right?"

Jenny nodded, wiped her face with her sleeve, then ran to the barn so she didn't have to watch him leave.

"Ye'll be back when I say ye can," Ian said plainly, the

rage gone now that he was certain he got his way.

I ran up to Scout and gave him a big hug. I whispered in his ear, "Did you take some food? It doesn't look like he has anything in his bag."

"Aye. Jenny gave me all those pro-teen bars, as she calls 'em. She said she could make more. Dinna worry about Da and me. I'll do my best to make sure he doesna get in *serious* trouble."

"You do that. And you know you're welcome to stay with us at any time, right?"

"Aye, but someone has to watch out fer him. Maybe by spendin' some time with Da, I can teach *him*."

"We can only hope and pray," I said, and kissed him on the cheek.

Wallace came up and shook Scout's hand. "Be careful out there. We'll be praying for you."

Ian rolled his eyes and snorted. "Let's go. We've tarried here long enough."

And then they were gone, neither of them looking back, although Scout did slip his hand behind his back to give me a surreptitious wave good-bye.

Yes, Scout would be fine. It's that father of his who

needed to learn a lesson or twelve.

2 Not So Modern Communications

Late November 1783
Backwoods North Carolina

Clunk! Clunk!

"What was that?" I called out the door.

Jenny popped her head around the corner. "I was trying to put my telegraph wire up on the eave, but the end I tied the rock to keeps falling down. I didn't have any wire, so I used rope. Then," my blonde pre-teen daughter sighed in exasperation, "I didn't have enough rope, so I used pieces of rag that I tore into strips so I could make my own. I thought I had enough to reach the whole way," she added a snort of frustration, "but it's still too short. James said that where he was from, you could send messages over wires, but since we don't have any wire—he said that's made of copper or some other kind of metal, albumen, I think—I have to use what I can find around here."

"I think you mean aluminum. That's very resourceful of you, sweetheart, but I think that it needs to be real metal

11

wire, not cloth or sisal."

I saw her scowl of frustration wasn't going to vanish by itself anytime soon, so I tried to think of a way to bring a smile back to my very own 18th century Pippy Longstockings. And, boom, just like one of Jenny's rocks landing on the roof, there it was.

"We may not have wire, but since you've already strung the rope and rag cording from here to James and Leah's, all you need to do is tie a bell onto each end. If you need to get their attention, just pull the cord on your end and their bell will ring. If they need you, they can do the same thing. But we'll need two bells."

"Really? Oh, oh!" Jenny exclaimed, bouncing up and down. "And I can still use that Morris Code that James has been teaching me. Do you know it? It's dots and dashes, he said, but they're actually just short and long noises. We can use clangs and claa-angs. I almost have the alphabet memorized already!"

"First, it's Morse code and second, I think you'd be better off having short signals. How about we only ring the bell when we want someone from the other house to come give us a hand. Your father can be one clang, I'll be two, and you can be three. When we call over to their house, James can be one clang, Leah can be two, and I can't see a reason why we'd need to ring for their babies. Most likely, they'll be ringing for you. Now, how many clangs would that be?"

"Three! But we're going to have to find a couple of bells first. I don't think we have any around here."

"Well, I'm sure your father will find something. Or James can make something."

My daughter Leah and son-in-law James had arrived from the twenty-first century two years ago and now lived shouting distance away from our humble home in 1783 North Carolina. I'd been here almost a year longer than they had, and they had adapted quickly, too. James was handy with re-creating modern conveniences with what we had on hand. Ceiling fans and solar water heaters were his greatest achievements, but he bragged that he was just getting started.

"Are you sure you'll be all right watching all these babies by yourself?" Jenny asked, bringing me out of my reverie on how so much had changed in such a short time.

"Yes, dear. I was doing most everything by myself before you came into our lives. I mean, your father helped me and so did Granny, but I think it's time you got a break. Think of it as a Daddy-Daughter date."

I was having a difficult time convincing my precocious adopted daughter that I could handle three toddlers for half a day. Actually, Wallace was doing me a favor. Feeding and keeping track of our triplets was a breeze compared to playing the living, breathing internet search engine of 1783 for the most inquisitive girl in the state. She pretty much grew up without parents, and her now deceased elder brothers who had reared her had been about one shoelace shy of being feral. There was plenty for her to learn, and she was a quick study, but I wished she wouldn't try to achieve a college-level education less than a year after learning simple math and how to read.

"What's a date for daddies and daughters? I've never heard of it. I know Daddy is my daddy, and I'm his daughter now, and I know the date of Christmas is in fourteen days, but no one told me about a Daddy-Daughter date. Is it a holiday? Oh, and am I supposed to make him a gift or do something special for it?"

Saved by the clomp, clomp of my husband's boots coming up the porch steps.

"How's my favorite middle daughter doing, Jenny?" Wallace said and braced himself for her linebacker hug.

When it didn't appear, he knelt down to accept a more sedate hug and squeeze from the forlorn Jenny. He stood up and looked to me, then nodded toward Jenny. 'Is there something wrong?' I shook my head, 'She's all right,' so he turned his attention back to her.

"Are you ready to go to town?" He stroked her head from the crown down to her ear. "The weather is clear, but it's still cold, so grab an extra scarf."

While she rummaged through the box of scarves and mittens, my husband turned to me. "Are you sure you'll be all right watching all these babies by yourself?"

"You two! What? Did you get together and memorize lines or something?" I looked over at the two of them, standing elbow-to-shoulder, blank looks on their faces. "It's like memorizing Bible verses or poems or something. Yes, the young ones and I will keep each other entertained, I'm sure. If nothing else, we'll take that rag ball you made and go outside and play catch until they're worn out."

"Or you're worn out. I'm sure glad they're still taking naps. I'm hoping Mr. Gibson gives me a good price for the chest. It's going to be tight…"

"But we always manage, right?"

Wallace leaned down and kissed me on the lips, ignoring the tittering giggles of Jenny. "We'll manage, I'm sure. Now, if he's in a good mood and his arthritis isn't bothering him, I may have a couple extra coins. Is there anything you need or want, other than the flour, salt, and cornmeal?"

"Surprise me," I said. "Whatever you bring me will be appreciated."

3 Skunky Slippers

Wallace stepped outside and looked up, gauging the weather by the breeze on his face one last time before they left. The air was still dry and barely moving. Fair weather for another day, at least. Two weeks ago, they had experienced an early snow, but all that remained of the six-inch fall were wind-polished icy patches in the shady spots under a few trees and dense bushes.

He climbed onto the buckboard seat next to Jenny. "So, are you ready to go?" he asked. "And will you be warm enough?" and tucked in the two cream-colored woolen blankets she had laid over her lap.

"I'm fine," she answered and scooted closer to him, "but you need to keep warm, too," and proceeded to rearrange the woven coverings to include his legs, too.

"Thank you,' he said. "Now, the sooner we leave, the sooner we'll be back to rescue your mother from your siblings." He flicked the reins over the horse's back and headed into town to sell his latest creation: a sugar chest.

The cherrywood locking cabinet on stubby little legs would serve a dual purpose for its new owner. Not only would it make a secure storage area for both white and dark sugars in the two-compartment chest itself, the top was slanted to provide a writing desk. He might be able to get more money from it if he could wait to find the right buyer himself, but Joseph Gibson, the storekeeper, had a better chance of selling it in a hurry. Christmas was nearing, and although they had everything they needed for the next few months, provisions would be meager or non-existent if they had a late spring.

"What's a Daddy-Daughter date?" Jenny asked, gazing up at him, sure that he could explain it better than Mommy had.

"I'm not sure, but it sounds like it could be fun."

"Mommy said that's what we're doing now, going on a Daddy-Daughter date. Does it have to be today, or can it be on any day?"

Wallace rolled his eyes. Evie usually gave him forewarning when she told Jenny about a subject or event that was from her previous life in the 21st century. Right now, he'd just 'wing it,' as she called it.

"*Any* time you and I are alone together, especially away from home, can be a Daddy-Daughter date. Now, after I get paid for the sugar chest, we may have a few extra coins. I was going to buy a gift for your mother, but I don't know what she wants or needs. Can you think of anything?"

Jenny tipped her head from one side to the other, sighed, started to speak up, then sighed again. "She keeps telling me she has everything she needs. Every once in a while, she says she wishes she had another set of hands, but then she says that's what you and I are for."

"I'm sure we'll find something. If not, we'll save that money for later. You do remember what we told you about money, right?"

"Money isn't everything, but it's necessary when we can't barter or trade, build or scavenge, hunt or fish for what we do need." Jenny paused and cleared her throat. "Is that a good enough answer?"

"Yes, I think you have it down." He looked down at her and saw she was grimacing in discomfort. "Are you all right?"

"It hurts my throat when I talk 'cause the air's so cold." She re-wrapped her scarf around her neck. "I guess I'll just stop talking then."

The two rode along in a comfortable silence for an hour, Wallace designing another piece of furniture in his head, this one a kitchen cabinet with a removable basin in it, with room for a hand pump at the side.

"Hey, look! What kind of animal is that?" Jenny asked, pulling on his coat sleeve to get his attention.

Wallace leaned forward and squinted to focus on the creature traveling on the wagon wheel-rutted path that was considered the road to Gibsonville. It appeared to be a massive bear, but the fur was mottled and the gait was that of a stumbling man. "I think someone is carrying a large load. Maybe we can offer him a hand."

"Or a ride," Jenny said, and scooted closer to him to make more room.

The man beneath the bulk of bundled furs heard the crunching of the wheels on the road and stepped aside to allow the wagon to pass.

Wallace slowed the horse, then pulled up beside him and stopped the wagon. The Native American man was about the same age as he was, broad-shouldered, but thin, and definitely ready to collapse. "Hey there, friend. Are you in need of assistance?"

The man nodded, then grimaced as he shifted his load.

Wallace jumped down and helped remove the rawhide-tied bundle of furs from his back. "You're welcome to ride in front with my daughter and myself. The bench is wide and we were just about to have a bite to eat. We'd be pleased if you'd join us."

Jenny had anticipated the scenario and had already removed the satchel of food from the storage chest under the buckboard seat, or 'bonnet' as James called the modification he had made. She held her bundle close, making sure the tall man had room to sit.

It took two tries before the traveler could pull himself up to the bench seat. Jenny looked at her father and he glanced back, glad that, for once, Jenny didn't make a comment about the obvious. The man was probably weak from hunger and exhausted from toting the heavy load.

After the man was settled in, Jenny pulled the second blanket from her lap. "My name is Jenny, and I think you'd be more comfortable if you wrapped this around your shoulders. I'll bet your back is cold now that you don't have all those furs on it, huh?"

"Thank you, Jenny," the blue-lipped man said, unable to

cover the quiver in his voice. He settled into the blanket, still warm from her body heat. "My name is Samuel."

"And this is my daddy, Wallace Pomeroy-Hart. He wasn't always my daddy, but he is now. We're on a Daddy-Daughter date today, but it's all right if you come with us. Sometimes a party is more fun when you have other people, especially new people. We live that way," she said, and sat forward so she could point behind her. "Where do you live?"

Wallace opened his mouth to tell her to let their new friend rest but remained mute when he saw the gentle man smile. He squinted and looked up at the sun to get his bearings. "A few days walk in that direction. I've come to trade for food for my tribe."

"I'm sure Mr. Gibson will be fair with you. I'm bringing that chest in to him," Wallace tipped his head to point to his creation. "He won't be buying it for himself, but he is acquainted with some of the more affluent families in the area. He said that sugar chests are becoming very popular but are hard to find." Wallace saw the confused look on the man's face. "Sugar is quite valuable, so the families who can afford it, keep it under lock and key to keep servants, or whomever, from stealing it."

Jenny saw the confused look on Samuel's face. "I couldn't figure it out either. Who would want to steal? I mean, if a man's working for someone, and he stole from him, wouldn't they ask him to leave because of it? And then he wouldn't have a job or *anything!*"

Samuel smiled and nodded, then pulled the blanket closer around his neck.

"Hey!" Jenny said, sitting upright and turning toward the wayfarer. "I just remembered something. My brothers—not the brothers I have now, but my other brothers who are in heaven—used to take their furs to the man who lived just before you get to the store. I'll show you where 'cause we're going to ride right past it. But I think we ought to let you off there instead of going to the store. You see, Mr. Gibson—he's the storekeeper, remember?—sells the furs you trade to him to someone else. His name is Karl Something-or-other, but Mr. Karl's good enough. Now, the first price he offers you is not the price you want to take. He gives you a low price right away, but he doesn't expect you to take it. Just shake your head when he says it and frown. Tell him you know you can get a better price."

Jenny paused in her instructions, realizing that Samuel

was not likely to haggle when it came to prices. He barely spoke at all. "Maybe you'd better just shake your head and walk to the door. He'll get the idea. He really wants skins. Not many folks have skins for sale this time of year. They're going out trapping now, not selling. Asides, I saw that you had quite a few furs in there that were already stretched and tanned. He'll pay more for them. Or he should. Don't let him cheat you. I know you need the money for food for your mother and sisters and all those other folks in your tribe. You can tell him that. Or just shake your head and walk to the door. He'll give you the money, and then you can come to Mr. Gibson's store to buy what you need."

Samuel looked down at Jenny and said, "I didn't tell you about my mother and sisters…"

"Jenny has a vivid imagination sometimes," Wallace said, and gave her a stern look, letting her know she had just revealed too much of what she 'saw' about Samuel. "But she's right about the tanner. See him first."

"Oh, and we have about," Jenny looked up to the sun, then shut her eyes as she calculated the time of day from the sun's position, "another hour to go before we get there." She reached into the satchel on her lap and took out a napkin and spread it on her lap like a tablecloth.

"I made sandwiches for everyone this morning before we left. We make flatbread sometimes, and put cheese and shredded cabbage on it, then roll it up! It's really good. Here's yours," she handed the tortilla-wrapped meal to Samuel, "and here's yours, Daddy. And here's mine. It's smaller than those two because my hands are smaller. Actually, my whole body is smaller, so I don't need as much food to stay warm and strong and I think I'd better stop talking and eat."

Wallace could tell by the confused look on Samuel's face that he'd never eaten anything like the 'wrapped' sandwich. "A bit different, but easy to handle when on the road," he said, then bit into it.

Samuel copied Wallace, biting into the end of the meal rather than starting in the middle as he thought he should. He chewed the unusual textured concoction, then smiled. "Good. Very good," he said. His stomach growled in agreement, and they all chuckled.

"Here's your drink, Samuel, and here's Daddy's and here's mine."

Jenny passed around the stoneware vessels that held some of the pressed apple cider she had helped put up two months ago. "*Slante!*" she toasted, then toped back a dribble. She put the stopper back in her bottle, then returned it to the lunch bag. "I'll finish it later," she said, then leaned closer to her father, and fell fast asleep.

***

Wallace pulled up to the small log cabin in front of the large clapboard structure that was the tanner's. The sudden cessation of movement wakened Jenny from her deep slumber. "Oh, we're here already. Can I come in and say hello to Mr. Karl, Daddy?"

"Go ahead. I'll help Samuel split this load up so Karl can see that many of these are tanned skins and hides, not just pelts."

Jenny rubbed the sleepy dust out of her eyes, then wrapped her lap blanket around her shoulders as a shawl. She stomped her feet loudly as she headed up the steps to the house to announce her presence. "Hello, Mr. Karl," she shouted. "It's me, Jenny. I brought you some good skins."

The scraping of wood on wood indicated that a door bolt was being removed. "Jenny? I thought you was dead?" he said, then scratched his head. "No, wait. I remember now. It was your brothers that died. You went to live with the healer's daughter and her husband or something like that."

Wallace walked up with half the load of furs over his shoulder, Samuel a step behind him with the rest of the pelts. "Greetings, Karl. Yes, I'm Jenny's father now, and this is Samuel. We have some mighty fine skins for you to look over. I noticed that some of these are prime and are already tanned and stretched, so should bring top dollar with your buyers. Less work for you, too. I'm sure you'll give him a fair price, but I must warn you, Jenny's already instructed him on how to deal with you."

Karl half laughed, half snorted at the remark. "Jenny, are you trying to take away my profits?" When he saw the quizzical look on her face, he changed his wording. "Jenny, are you trying to take coins out of my pocket and give them to someone else?"

"Only if he deserves them, and he does. Now, if you're not fair to him, I'll tell my brothers up in heaven to give you nightmares and scare the grasshoppers into your fields and mice into your cellar and turn your cider into vinegar and…and… Well, all sorts of evils will come your way if you cheat this man. He does have a mother and sisters and a few others to take care of still."

Karl's eyes widened in shock at what could almost be called a curse. Wallace saw his distress and tapped her on the shoulder, bringing her back to his side. "I'm sure Samuel and Mr. Karl can work out an agreement. Come on, I want to get to the store. I don't think it's going to rain or snow, but I don't want to be coming home in the dark, either."

***

Mr. Gibson the storekeeper was all smiles when he saw Wallace and Jenny walk in. "Did you get that sugar chest finished? I think I already have a buyer for it."

"It's just outside. Come take a look. Jenny, go ahead and see if you can find something for your mother. We'll be back shortly."

Jenny took her time looking at the bottles that held colored glass beads, toggles and buttons, the trays of buckles, all three bolts of fabric, then stopped. She found what she wanted: the larger jars that held candies. There were so many of them: four! She knew what most of them were from years ago when her brothers had spent all the money they earned from trapping that winter on candy. The brown ones were maple sugar candy and molasses pulls; the pure white ones, peppermint sticks; the yellow pieces lemon

28

sours, and it looked as if he even had marzipan. Her mouth watered in anticipation. She opened the door and looked outside at her daddy to see if Mr. Gibson was happy with the sugar chest. She jumped up and down with joy: both of them were all smiles. Maybe she'd get candy!

Samuel walked up to the two white men—Wallace, the tall, quiet young man who had given him a ride just as he was ready to collapse, and the other man, an older gentleman who must by the storekeeper, Mr. Gibson. He stopped ten feet away and waited for them to finish their discussion. They were transacting business and he didn't want to intrude or eavesdrop.

Mr. Gibson looked up from his inspection of the sugar chest and saw the half-breed Indian waiting patiently. "Wallace told me you'd be needing some supplies. Go on in out of the cold to wait. No use catching a chill. I'll be in shortly."

Samuel nodded that he understood, then walked up the two steps to the store, grinning. He had actually been invited in! Is this what it felt like to be an all-white man? Maybe he should have said thank you, but he didn't like to speak. He knew many English words, but still had trouble getting his tongue wrapped around some of their sounds. It was much easier to read and write their language than to speak it. He would, however, make sure he told Wallace how much he appreciated his help.

And Jenny. He'd thank her, too, for feeding him and offering him the cider that revived his spirit. And for warning Mr. Karl about the perils that would befall him if he didn't give him a fair price. The man was quick to give him more than he expected, then he swiftly amended it, offering him even more. Yes, with the hearty fare he had eaten and the cider, he now had the energy to return to the village with winter supplies. He suppressed a sigh of satisfaction but couldn't keep the corners of his mouth from lifting in appreciation. He might even be able to afford a mule if there was one in town, but he didn't think he'd be that fortunate. Still, it would make returning with the food much easier. It was a long walk back…

"Oh, hello, Samuel," Jenny said, then stepped away from the candies. "Karl did well by you, I can tell from your smile. He's a good man, but he gets greedy sometimes. Did you make a list for what you need or do you have it memorized?"

Samuel didn't understand all her words, but he did know

what he needed. He held out his coins to show her how much he had received.

"Ooh, he was *very* good to you. Here, let me show you around. This is where he keeps the flour, and over here in this barrel is the cornmeal, and…"

Jenny's tour of the little store was interrupted by an angry voice calling back from the opened door. "Get yer lazy arse up here before I have to kick it up the steps."

The grizzled man with the slouch hat pulled down over sprawling, matted hair and a greasy beard spotted with heaven-only-knew-what reached out and grabbed the small dark-haired woman by the arm. "Were ye raised in a barn? Nah. Not that lucky. Get in here. Yer lettin' all the warm air out."

The petite woman in the patched ankle-length buckskin dress shuffled in, stopping in front of the pot-bellied stove that heated the single-room store.

"Get away from that! Let the white folks get warmed up first." He pushed her aside and turned his back to the heat source. He realized he wasn't the only one in the room and turned his attention to Jenny. "Good day, little miss. Is that yer father out there?"

Jenny nodded, terrified of the man she'd just met. She didn't have to be psychic to sense the evil that was all about him. She shook her head to erase the unwanted mental images overloading her mind, of him beating and mistreating the Indian woman with him.

"Well, what is it? Is he yer pa or not?" the man bellowed.

Samuel came out from the shadows and stood beside her. "He's her father," he said, and glowered at the short dumpy man, crossing his arms in front of himself to let it be known that he was the girl's champion, and that her white father, his friend, was within shouting distance.

"Ooh, yer a tall one. Yer pa musta been a mighty big white man, him bein' able to build such a tall buck with one of them wee little squaws. Now, move aside. I have some goods to purchase." He snorted in derision at Samuel, "And the proprietor will want to see to my needs first since I'm using real coin, not wampum."

Samuel clenched his jaws. It wouldn't do his family any good if he let his temper out. One good punch to the mouth, and the man would lose the rest of his teeth. Or maybe he'd target the man's gut. One hard jab and he could push his fist all the way through to the man's spine. He'd reach in, pull it

32

out, and strangle him with it…

Jenny looked up and saw Samuel's face had turned scarlet. She could feel his righteous rage, but didn't want him to lose his temper and get in trouble. The white man was always right around here, even when it wasn't fair or just. "Come help me figure out what kind of candies these are," Jenny said, and urged him away from the arrogant bigot.

"I think I want to get my mother a peppermint stick," Jenny whispered to Samuel, trying to distract him. "You see, if Daddy gets enough money for the sugar chest, then we can get two. Then I can have one candy and share it with my little brothers and sister and my mother…"

She stopped in mid-thought and sniffed the air. "What's that smell?" she asked, looking around the room.

The pork-bellied white man roared out loud, laughing so hard, he broke wind. "That's her shoes. See?" He pointed to the woman's black and white striped raw pelt slippers, bound around her feet with strips of coarse-cut leather. "She went and lost her shoes, so I made her another pair. Ye'd think she'd be grateful, but she wouldn't wear them 'til I threw her others in the fire."

Samuel's back straightened, his chest puffed out in

anger, but he stayed where he was when he felt Jenny's hand on his arm, silently begging him to stand down.

The meek woman looked up at the handsome stranger, saw his rage, then said, "They'll do." She'd seen the man who owned her get mad before. It wouldn't do for him to get in another fight. And kill again. She glanced back at the man who was at least half Indian, ready to stand in her defense. Her master didn't fight fair, but he did make sure the other person would never come back at him again. She moved away from the door and inched closer to the fire.

"Ach, I guess ye can warm yer scrawny bones a bit. My arse is so warm now, it feels like it's afire."

Mr. Gibson and Wallace walked in and immediately started sniffing the air. "What's that smell?" the storekeeper asked.

The woman collapsed to the floor in tears. Jenny rushed to her side and started patting her back, telling her she'd be all right, to ignore everyone else in the room.

"It's her shoes!" Porkbelly said, and started laughing all over again. He finally regained his composure and looked at Mr. Gibson and Wallace. "It gets me to laughin' every time. Now, I have a lot of goods I need, so let's get to it."

Mr. Gibson looked from Wallace to the tall, silent Indian and said, "I'm sorry, sir. There are two gentlemen ahead of you. Wallace?"

"Here's the list of the foodstuffs," he said and gave it to Mr. Gibson, trying to ignore the crude comedian.

"What? Two gentlemen? I only see an overgrown farm boy and the leftovers from a soldier's carousing in the woods," then he began laughing again.

Wallace walked up to the crude, dumpy man, just inches away, and stared down, the man's upturned face a full head and a half below his. He had no intention of telling the man that he wasn't common-born, that until a few years past, he had been a titled landowner in England, but he would use his Lord of the Manor demeanor to his advantage. "Am I to assume that you intentionally shod this young woman with the untanned skins of polecats?"

"Aye," he crowed, and started to laugh again. "Ain't that a hoot?" then his merriment faded. He wasn't afraid of the big half-breed Indian. He could, and had, gotten away with whatever he wanted as long as he was in civilization, but this tall white boy—who he had thought an underaged and overgrown dirt farmer—had the speech and manner of someone high born. He sucked back his merriment. This lad might be connected with the constables. It would be best to keep on this one's good side.

"Well, at the time, it was all I had," he said with feigned sincerity.

"Am I to believe that you provided your wife with fetid vermin pelts to cover her delicate skin?"

Porkbelly started to laugh aloud, then thought better of it, but couldn't suppress a chuckle. "My wife? This ain't my wife. I paid a full dollar for her upriver a year ago last spring. The chief said she couldn't get a babe in her belly, so was worthless. I could do what I wanted with her."

Wallace's eyes widened in shock, but he quickly blinked back his rage. He glanced over at Samuel and saw that Jenny was now at his side, her hand on his arm, effectively holding the livid man down with her gentle touch.

"I'll tell you what, mister," Wallace said congenially, then changed into his commanding officer tone when he saw the smug look on the ornery man's face. "Mister... I'm sorry. We haven't been introduced. However, names are not important in this case, so I'll just refer to you as Mr. Smith. Therefore, Mr. Smith, since you paid one full dollar for this woman a year and a half ago, I'll relieve your burden by taking this woman with me and I'll give you back that full dollar. No deductions for the wear and tear she seems to have incurred," he looked down at her red swollen ankles, "and lack of proper footwear." He held out an uncut silver Spanish dollar and offered his other hand to seal the transaction. "Do we have an agreement?"

The man now called Mr. Smith looked at the money, then over to the squaw, huddled on the ground, the scrawny young blonde who couldn't be much more than twelve now back trying to comfort her. "Why not? She can't cook worth a lick, and she's not much better at keeping me warm at night. But be careful! She bites when really riled." He shrugged one arm out of his heavy coat, then pulled up his sleeve to show the viscous bite mark on his inner arm, thick red streaks going out in all directions from it.

Mr. Smith pulled his arm back inside his coat, then grabbed for the money. Wallace had seen the intent in his eyes and held the coin high. He vigorously shook the man's blood poisoned right hand to complete the deal in front of witnesses, then handed him the coin. "I hear tell that the ordinary in the next town has saddle of mutton and sweetbreads along with the finest ale in the state. You could buy yourself a *very* fine meal there."

"Aye, and maybe someone to keep me warm tonight." He looked at Mr. Gibson, the man who had denied him priority service. "And I'm sure their stores are stocked with more provisions there than you have here. Farewell, Annie. I'd like to say it's been a pleasure, but as you and I both know, it hasn't." He tipped his filthy slouch hat to the store owner and Wallace, then shuffled out the door, letting loose another of his raucous laughs.

The room was suddenly empty and silent. "Now, then," Mr. Gibson said to break the bubble of gloom, "Didn't you want to get a few more items, Wallace?"

"I was going to have Jenny pick out some cloth and threads for her mother, but I'm afraid my funds have dwindled. I think we'll have enough left over for some candy, though. Do you think she'd like that, sweetheart?"

Jenny looked up from the dirt floor, still holding onto 'Annie.' "Mommy said she's always had a sweet tooth, so I think a peppermint stick will make her happy. Maybe Father Christmas will bring us some cloth."

"Oh, it's just as well that you wait for the fabric, Wallace.

I had a shipment coming in from Calcutta by way of London, but it's been delayed. Check back after the first of the year," he said and winked.

Wallace turned to look behind him, trying to figure out why Gibson was winking, then sighed as he realized that his shipment would probably be in before Christmas.

"Here's your change for your purchases," the storekeeper said, dropping a few pieces of eight into Wallace's hand. He looked up and saw that his customer was about to protest—they both knew that he had given him the correct amount of money for the goods Gibson had gathered while the negotiating for Annie had transpired.

"You got the gentleman of the year discount for helping out the young lady there," Gibson said. He reached into the candy jar and pulled out three peppermint sticks and wrapped them in an old political flyer. "And here's a surprise for your ladies," nodding to Jenny and Annie, "and your wife. It's for…well, just because. Happy Christmas to you and your family."

Gibson turned his attention to the other man in the room, Samuel. "Now, sir, how may I help you."

"I'll be right back, Jenny," Wallace said. "I want to secure the food in the wagon, then I'll help you and Annie outside. Move closer to the stove so you can get extra warm. It's a long ride back and I think the wind is kicking up."

Jenny took the second scarf from around her neck and arranged it around the terrified young woman. "Welcome to our family, Annie. My mother said she wanted an extra pair of hands around the house, so I guess that's what she's getting. At least until it's spring. You don't *have* to stay with our family, but we want you to. Both my granny and sisters are healers, too, and maybe one of them can get the redness and swelling to go away on your feet. Oh, and here."

Wallace came in and watched as Jenny pulled her skirt up to her shins, unlaced and pulled off her boots. "I wore two pairs of stockings today because I'm wearing what my older sister Leah—she's not my blood sister 'cause I'm adopted, but she's my sister, just the same—what she calls hand-me-downs. They'll still fit me with just one pair of stockings, though. We can toss those polecat skins in the burn pile and you can wear my other pair. These are real woolen stockings. They kinda look odd because they had to be patched where my heal rubbed a hole in one of them, but they're still warm."

Jenny had been removing her socks as she recited the story of why she had a spare pair and what her relationship was to her older sister. "Oh, my! That's gotta hurt!" she said when she pulled off Annie's footwear. "Goodness! I didn't know toes could turn black."

"Go ahead and put your extra socks on her, Jenny, but be very gentle," Wallace said. "She has what's called frostbite on her toes. I'm sure your mother, sister, or Granny knows what to do for it. In the meantime, we'll keep them warm and covered."

Wallace waited for Mr. Gibson to come out of the back room with an empty flour sack for Samuel's order. "Thank you again, for your help, Mr. Gibson. I'll see you in a few weeks maybe."

Gibson winked and said, "Sooner might be better. Be safe, and congratulations on the new addition to your family."

Wallace watched as Jenny finished putting the stockings on the dark-haired young woman. Annie's eyes were wide and vacant, like the shell-shocked soldiers he'd seen at the front when he was an officer in His Majesty's Army. Suddenly, the glassiness faded and warmth came into her eyes. He followed her gaze. Samuel was looking at her, his

41

eyes narrowed in concern.

Wallace walked up and placed a hand of reassurance on the man's shoulder. "She'll be safe, my friend. She's a free person, not a slave or an indentured servant, and may leave at any time. However, right now I think it's best that we take her to the healer. She'll be warm and safe with my family."

Wallace watched as Samuel breathed a big sigh of relief, then added a terse, "Thank you," and gave a nervous sliver of a smile to Annie.

"Would you help me get her to the wagon, Samuel? Just grab one elbow and I'll get the other. I don't want her feet to touch the ground."

The two men ported the scared, but unresisting, woman to the wagon. Samuel held her in his arms while Wallace got in the wagon. Wallace patted the side of the seat where she was to ride and Samuel handed her up to him. Yes, there was a definite attraction between the two, but he knew that Samuel didn't have much, if anything, to offer the young woman.

"Feel free to come visit her any time you'd like. Jenny gave you the general location of our home. We're not difficult to find. Just look for the building shaped like this." Wallace put his fingertips together to indicate the shape of the tepee that James was building as his final home.

"Before we leave, Mr. Gibson," Jenny said, "I want to thank you for helping us. I know you didn't have to buy that sugar chest..."

"Oh, pish posh. He's a fine craftsman and, mark my word, his works will be in great demand soon. But before you leave," he went behind the counter, reached into the candy jar, held all the peppermint sticks to the side, then poured the crumbs out onto a scrap of paper. "Here's some traveling sweets for all of you. The bits are too small to sell, but taste just as good."

Jenny accepted the treasure packet with a smile, a giggle, then a big hug. "Thank you!"

He leaned down and whispered, "You make sure you're nice to that young woman. She's had a rough time. This wasn't the first time those two have been in my store. The last time was summer, though. If you and your father hadn't said something, well," he rubbed his chin in deep thought. "I don't know what my wife woulda done if I brought home a full-grown woman to stay with us, but I woulda dealt with her fussing and hollering rather than let him keep abusing her like that. Not even letting her have a tanned hide so she could make her own shoes, and him having so many of them."

"We'll be good to her. Oh, and I didn't know what to do with those old polecat shoes of hers. They're still on the floor by the stove."

"Now, don't you worry about it. I'll have a bonfire going sometime soon. I'll toss them onto it when the wind starts blowing the right direction. Now git before your pa leaves without you."

"Yes, sir," Jenny said and bounced out the door. He was her pa and everyone in this town knew it. Finally, a real father.

And maybe another sister.

4 Chasing Christmas

Late November 1783

"Mom, remember when I was little and always asked, 'When's it going to be Christmas,' and you'd say, 'There's no sense in chasing Christmas. It'll get here when it's time.'"

Leah's face fell as soon as the words were out of her mouth. "Crap. Sorry, Mom. Well, if you *could* remember anything, I'm sure that's one of the things you'd remember."

I chuckled at her embarrassment. "You know what? That's the sort of thing I really *want* you to remind me about. That's a sweet memory. Now, if you can give me enough like those, I won't care that I have amnesia. I doubt that the wee three or even Jenny will ever have that gimme-gimme attitude, though, because Christmas isn't a big commercial deal in this day and age..."

I looked back at her to see if she was smiling yet or not. She was. "Doesn't it sound weird? 'In this day and age.' How many people can actually claim to have lived in two centuries that were separated by a third one?"

"As far as I know," she replied, multitasking nursing her young son while corralling her daughter between her outstretched legs, "it's just you, me, James, and Sarah. But you do remember what a madhouse they made Christmas into, right?"

"Yup. Halloween costumes were barely off the racks and then colored lights, ornaments, and wrapping goodies fought for floor space with toys and gizmos that were gifted then tossed in the garbage after a month or less."

"If they were even used at all. And the clothes! Remember ugly Christmas sweaters? Who thought of that?" Leah shuddered, disturbing young River. "It's okay, sweetie. Finish eating. I want to visit with your grandma a while longer." She looked up. "When do you think Jenny and Wallace will be back?"

I looked out at the sun, setting low in the corner of the southern window. "I hope soon. Dinner's ready now, so if you want to eat early, go ahead. I had half a jar of pickles before you came over, so I'm set for a while."

"Mom," she asked slowly and gently. "Do you think you're pregnant again?"

I snorted and shook my head. "Nope. Period started

today, just like clockwork. If you don't see a moon, that means it's my time of the month. I really don't *need* to have another child. I mean, Leo, Judah, and Wren are two-and-a-half years old now and potty trained, so a new one wouldn't be too hard to handle."

"Another one? Ah, come on, Mom. You had me as a single, then the triplets. Aren't you due for twins?"

"Bite your tongue!" I said, then took it down a notch. "No, whatever the Lord decides to give us will be fine. I know Wallace says he couldn't love you or the others any more, even if he had sired you, but I really do want to have one of his children. I can't believe my luck…"

Leah interrupted. "Blessing!"

"Right. I can't believe how blessed I was to find a father for them, even before they were born." I shook my head and images of my past relationship with my first husband rattled up, down, and sideways. "I really and truly can't imagine being married to Ian, what my life would be like now." I saw that she didn't know why I had brought it up. That part of my life had been over for more than three years.

"Ian came and took Scout away this spring," I said. "He's probably on another one of his vengeance quests and wants to train his son in the fine art of retribution. That poor boy. It shouldn't be the son trying to keep the parent out of trouble. And Scout's not even a teenager yet. Or at least I don't think he is. Still, he doesn't even have a whisker and he's trying to keep that…that ornery bugger…"

I looked around, back in the present, ready to dismiss the woulda-coulda-shoulda issues and control who and what I could. "What are my wee three up to now, anyhow?"

"James whipped up some pieces of thick paper then stitched a bunch of them together into a book. He colored the pages with all sorts of weird homemade inks. Your three are under that blanket in the corner, taking turns 'reading' it to each other."

"He put words in it, too?"

"Nope. He made images that we might recognize but told them they had to make up their own stories for the pictures. Seems to be keeping them busy."

Leah stood up suddenly, releasing her daughter from Mommy jail and bringing her son up with her to look out the window. "They're here," she said and sat back down. A split second later, she popped up to look outside again. "It looks like there's three of them, though. We got company. I'd better get myself together. Here, hold onto your grandson a minute. Oh, and he needs burped, too."

Wallace walked in, saw that I had the baby, and asked, "Leah, would you give me a hand?"

Leah looked around, made sure her daughter wasn't in harm's way, gave me a wide-eyed 'What now?' look, and left to help her stepfather.

The door had barely shut when Jenny burst in. "Mommy, Mommy! Oh, there you are. Do we have any hot water?"

"Um, it's winter. I always have hot water on. We don't have coffee or tea, though."

Jenny shook her head. "I don't mean to drink. I mean for a bath. Or a part of a bath. We got a new friend, maybe even another sister for me!" Jenny brought her boisterous attitude down to a whisper, "But she stinks. I think she wants to get rid of the polecat smell, too."

Jenny ran out the door, hollering to her father as she zipped past him. "I'll go get the wash tub!" and disappeared, skirts hiked high as she sprinted to the barn.

"Thanks, Leah, I think I got her," Wallace said, then turned toward the house. "I just didn't want her to be frightened, a strange man carrying her inside a house she's never been to. I hoped that seeing another woman would make her less tense."

I stepped out onto the porch and saw my husband leaving the wagon, walking towards me, carrying a Native American woman in his arms, Jenny's scarf around her neck. Neither seemed to notice that her buckskin dress had slipped up nearly to her knees, revealing the brightly patched socks I had darned only last night.

"Well, I got you a surprise," Wallace said weakly. "Would you clear a place in front of the fire for her."

I rushed ahead of him and shoved the stools the young ones sat on at dinner into the corner and tossed down the 'sitting' blanket we used in the evenings during story time.

Clunk! Clunk!

Jenny hollered, "Can someone get the door?" and kicked it. "We got our arms full." She turned to her father, "You can go ahead of me, Daddy. She's heavier and I don't want you to drop her."

I opened the door and was overwhelmed by the stench. I swallowed my gag reflex, then stepped outside, away from the pair, and took a deep breath of fresh air before coming back in to the *eau de skunk*.

Skunk! I just remembered. Not a defining 'I got my memory back' moment, but another one of those random but welcomed facts that helped all of us, especially those who were born in the 18th century. "Jenny, before you take your shawl off, would you go to the cellar and bring up as many jars of tomatoes as you can?"

Jenny grabbed one of the baskets I had made before the wee three were born from the corner and asked, "Are you sure you want to bring as many as I can carry?"

"All right. Bring me four quarts. That ought to do it."

Wallace placed the small woman on the quilt at the hearth, waiting until I had finished my request before making introductions. I don't think it mattered, though. She looked like she was in shock. Or maybe she was just terrified. Either way, I was the hostess and even if I wasn't, I wanted this frightened person to relax and feel safe.

"Evie, this is Annie. Annie, this is my wife, Evie."

The fear factor dropped from a full ten to about eight at the word 'wife.' I saw it and so did Wallace.

"You've already met one of our daughters, Jenny. This another daughter, Leah, and her family: Bibby Liz and young River."

Well, I'll say one thing for Annie: she didn't have to voice a question to ask it. At this point, I decided not to elaborate on how I—who looked to be 20 years old—could be the mother of someone who was a few years older. Instead, I just smiled at her and nodded. "Yes, those two are my grandchildren."

The wee three had come to watch the addition to the household, but were holding their tongues, figuratively. They were, however, holding their noses, literally.

"And these are my three youngest: Leo, Judah, and Wren. Say hello, children."

"Hello," they all mumbled through hands covering their noses.

"Let's go back and read," Wren said. "It's my turn because I wasn't finished when we came over to see... Mommy, what's her name?"

"I'm sorry. Children, this is Annie." I looked to Wallace and made a wild spousal supposition. "She's going to be staying with us for a while."

"All right," they chorused, then ran back to their corner, this time the blanket pulled over their heads.

I knew they couldn't 'read' in the dark, but they were

quiet under the quilt and weren't asking questions. Wow! Two mini miracles!

"Will Sarah be back soon?" Wallace asked. "I'm afraid she has frostbite on her feet. I'm not sure what to do, but I know what not to do: walk on them."

"I got this," Leah said. She unconsciously put the back of her hand up to her nose. "Wallace, why don't you put the children in the wagon and take them to my place for a bit. James should be done with his project by now. The little ones already ate, and Mom and I can hold off for a while." She gave him a stern 'I'm the nurse in charge' look, but she really didn't need to. Getting the children out of the house was a smart idea.

Jenny pushed the door open and came in with her half-filled basket. "I got the saucy tomatoes. I didn't think you'd want the lumpy ones." She set them down next to the washtub, then moved closer to her father and the door that he had left cracked open to allow fresh air in.

"Come on, children. Jenny, would you help me gather everyone together. Let's jump in the wagon since the horse is still hitched to it. I'll unload the supplies when we get back. You can hold River and keep Bibby Liz in line. You other

53

three are in charge of yourselves. Stay in the wagon and don't even look over the edge, all right?"

"Yes, sir," they chorused, then giggled. "Did we do that right, like we're in the militia?" asked Leo.

He rolled his eyes at their role playing. "Yes, soldiers. Now, march to the back of the wagon and prepare to deploy!"

5 Cleaning Day

It was an arduous task, trying to bathe an unresponsive person, but Leah had been a skilled nurse in her previous life in the 21st century and taking care of semi-lucid people was as she said, 'Just like riding a bicycle. You just have to know when to turn and when to stop.'

Leah poured one quart of the tomato sauce into a wooden bowl, then add two ladlesful of hot water to it. "Only time will tell if this will work. In the meantime, let's see if we can get the gag factor under control. Stink and small homes in the wintertime don't go well together. Even if this only works a little, anything is better than nothing. The poor dear."

Well, we soaked her feet in the tomato sauce bath, scrubbing as gently as we could to remove the traces of fur, dirt, grime and essence of polecat from between her healthy toes, just dabbing around the blackened tips of her big toes, but the stench remained.

"I'm sorry we put you through so much discomfort, Annie," Leah said, as she rinsed her hands in the basin of clear water. "I hate to say it, but let's try good old-fashioned soap." She then turned to me and said under her breath, "Too bad we don't have new-fashioned detergent, baking soda, and hydrogen peroxide. That's what we used for the Boy Scouts that year they cornered a skunk. One spray doused eight boys!"

Clomp, clomp, clomp!

It was Jenny.

"Before you scold me for not staying with Daddy and my brothers and little sister, James said that he and Daddy were big men and could manage the five little ones by themselves. Then James said you'd probably do better with his new all-purpose body wash and shampoo than with tomato sauce." Jenny produced a spring-topped glass bottle with a creamy white product in it. "Oh, and he said you could add this to the rinse water, too. But just a drop or two 'cause it's real portent."

"Potent," I corrected, taking the small vial from her. "That means strong." I uncorked it and took a whiff. "Whoo-ee! He's right there."

"I can smell it from here. Where'd he get oranges?" Leah asked.

"I helped him gather the fruit down by the river. I told him we called them hedge apples, but that they weren't really apples, and that the squirrels liked to eat the seeds..."

Jenny noticed me shaking my head.

"I guess I'll tell you about our harvest trip later. So, if Daddy and James are fine taking care of the babies, can I stay and help with Annie? I know I just met her, but I sorta miss her already." She turned to Annie. "Did you miss me, too?"

Annie gave Jenny a weak smile, the first indication that we'd had that she understood any of what was going on.

Jenny took the bottle of shampoo/body wash and uncapped it, offering it to Annie to sniff. "How'd you like to smell like this?" she asked, pointing to the tub that she'd brought in, but we hadn't used.

Annie nodded, then scooted forward and lifted up her dress. "Burn it," she said, scowling. "It's not mine." She proceeded to pull the wretched garment off over her head, then flung it toward the fire, missing the flames by a foot.

The pungent aroma of a body that hadn't been washed in ages was far worse than the skunk odor. I realized that maybe it wasn't just the polecat slippers that reeked. Her body was streaked with dirt and grime. Either *he* hadn't let her bathe or she intentionally stayed dirty so he'd keep away from her. Regardless, she needed a bath.

She sat there, naked and unashamed, and stared at the sweat and dirt-stained buckskin dress, too far away from the flame to burn.

"Here," I said, and handed her the poker. "Go ahead and burn it now while the fire is high. Send your old life to hell."

Annie's eyes misted up and she sniffed back her tears. "Go," she twisted the torn and patched dress onto the end of the fire tool, "to," tossed it into the blaze, "hell," then repositioned it in the flame, jamming it between the two large ash-covered orange logs. She took a deep breath as the flames roared up, a new stink permeating the air. "Gone."

Leah poured some of the body wash into a bowl and added hot water. "Do you want to help, Jenny? I think she's more comfortable with you."

Jenny took one of the fresh cloths and swirled it around the water, bringing the sweet orange smell into our immediate area. "I'll get your back for you, Annie. Go ahead and watch all your bad old memories go to the devil…or whatever Indians call him. You're living with us now. We don't know anything about you but your name, but you're part of our family now and we love you and care for you and will protect you…"

Annie reached up and covered Jenny's hand with hers. "My name." She looked to all of us in turn and began her narrative, using her hands to embellish her words.

"I'm called Annie. It sounds good when you say it, but that wasn't always my name." Eyes squinted and mouth pursed in anger, she suddenly spat into the fire. "*He,*" indicating a big belly, "made a joke about what the…the…" She paused, searching for the English word, then put three fingers behind the top of her head like a headdress.

"The chief?" Jenny asked. "The man in charge?"

Annie nodded. "Our old chief dead. The new one stupid. He much liked the white man's drink." She held her hand up, mimed guzzling liquor, wiped her mouth with the back of her hand, then sighed in satisfaction, a lopsided grin pasted on her face.

Then her clench-jawed anger returned. "*He* showed up with a big bottle of whisky, looking for someone to," she mimed a trap closing with both hands.

"Run his trap lines?" Jenny asked, then dropped her

59

washcloth back in the basin to use both hands to talk. "Someone to set the traps, take the dead animals out, skin them, and get them ready for the tanner?" verifying all the steps in the process with both hands and words.

Annie nodded, then whimpered. "And keep him warm at night," hugging herself in demonstration. "Chief," she held three fingers behind her head, then nodded to Jenny to make sure she had the word right. Jenny gave her the go ahead, and she resumed. "Chief pointed to three women and ask which one he want."

"*He* said 'any' woman would do. That's why he call me Annie. But he say 'Eny.' The way you say it is pretty," she said and smiled. It wasn't pronounced the same, so evidently didn't bother her now.

Her smile left as she continued. "Chief pointed to me. 'Take her. She no good at making baby.'"

Annie pointed to the marks on her belly. "No baby for me," sad at her words. Then she straightened up, proud. "I no want he*'s* baby in me, but he try." She shuddered at the memory.

Jenny had finished washing Annie's back and arms, and now knelt at her feet to wash her legs. "You'll have a baby one day," she said, looking up until Annie returned her gaze. "I know it."

Annie shrugged her shoulder in disbelief, then pointed to Leah. "The," she mimed mixing potions and applying them to her feet.

"Healer," Jenny and Leah said at the same time.

"Healer tried to make belly good for baby." She leaned back so we could clearly see the marks on her abdomen. Apparently, someone had 'cut' fertility symbols into her to increase her chances of having a child.

"Oh, my God," escaped my lips before I could stop.

"But now you're with us. You're safe and we won't cut you. But you *will* have a baby one day," Jenny repeated.

Jenny rinsed and re-soaped up the washcloth. "Here, you wash your lady parts," putting the cloth in front of her own crotch, then handing it to her, "And when you're done, I'll wash your hair," then flipped her hair back and forth like a shampoo commercial model.

Annie put the cloth up to her nose and smiled. "Stink good," she said, then her smile turned into eyebrow-narrowed determination, diligent in her cleansing ordeal, making sure the washcloth was thoroughly rinsed before dipping it into the soapy water. The closer she got to completion, the more relaxed her face and attitude. Finally, she rinsed the rag one final time, squeezed it out, then folded it neatly and set it on the tray next to the basin.

Jenny handed her a lap blanket to cover herself with. "Now, are you ready for your shampoo?" she asked, repeating her hair model swish and head turn.

Annie clutched the quilt to her chest and tried mimicking her, but she just didn't have the poise or the loose hair. All of us giggled, then felt embarrassed that maybe we were insulting her. Evidently not: she was stifling a giggle, too.

"I'll unbraid it first, then we can wash it and comb it out. Have you always worn your hair this way?" Jenny asked, flipping the end of one of her braids back and forth.

She nodded, then helped her new blonde friend unplait her hair, letting us know she was eager for a make-over.

While I looked for something more permanent for Annie to wear than a patchwork lap quilt, Leah dumped the basins of stinky water into the bushes outside the front door. It was too cold and windy to toss them any further. She came back in and set up the beauty salon, filling our drinking water ewer with warm water and setting the big wash tub behind the stool where Annie sat.

Jenny hummed a Christmas carol—Angels We Have Heard on High, I think—as she used her fingertips to work the first round of shampoo in. It was wash, rinse and repeat twice to cut the oil and dirt build up on her scalp. The wash tub caught the rinse water she poured over her head as Annie gazed at the ceiling. I never thought about it as I stared up with her, but our finished ceiling was probably strange to a young woman who was accustomed to living in mud structures or in the open air. She did look content, though. I guess the soapy water helped wash away her fear and angers, too.

While Jenny finished the beauty treatment, pulling a wide-toothed comb through Annie's long raven-black hair, Leah ran over to her house to check on the husbands and children. Or maybe that was just her excuse…

Five minutes later, she returned. She paused a moment to catch her breath, then looked at me with her impish schoolgirl grin before turning her attention to our guest. "Look what I have," she said to Annie who was now literally sitting pretty in front of the fireplace, wearing my clean cotton nightgown, her towel-dried hair hanging loose over her shoulders.

I'm sure Annie had seen a looking glass before, but I doubt she had seen her image lately. She really was beautiful. We watched as that slight shadow of a smile she had shared with us sporadically throughout the evening exploded into a full, ear-to-ear grin of appreciation. I really doubt she could have stopped it from getting so big, even if she had wanted to. She kept looking back at the mirror, touching her face and hair with appreciation, making sure it really was her.

"Pretty, huh?" Jenny asked.

"Pretty. Uh huh," she replied.

Clomp, clomp, clomp!

"Someone's here," I said, quickly scanning the room to make sure I had everything dangerous or spillable put aside and out of the wee ones' grasps. All we needed to do was empty the wash tub. Wallace spotted the need as soon as he stepped in the door, and two quick air-testing sniffs later, had both hands on it, ready to take it away.

"They were hungry again and Leah said you were at the point where we could come back home." He sniffed the air again. "It actually smells good in here." He looked at Annie who had turned her back on those coming in the house, facing the fire, timidly avoiding any socializing.

"Is that our Annie?" he asked me, knowing full well that it was. "Annie," he said to her, "Would you turn around so the children can see you? They told me they didn't get a chance to see you before we whisked them off to James and Leah's home."

Annie turned to face the three youngsters. "You're pretty!" Wren said. "I wish my hair was that long and pretty." She boldly walked up to her and sniffed her sleeve. "And you smell good, too." Wren turned to me, "Mommy, can I take a bath, too? I want to smell like Annie."

"Not me," Leo said, "I like smelling like a boy."

"Me, too," echoed Judah. "When can we eat? I'm hungry."

"You're always hungry," Wren said, "but this time, I'm hungry, too."

"Well, while you're feeding your babies, Mom, I'll go home and feed mine. I know James can put something together for Bibby Liz, but he's not equipped to feed River." She patted the top of one breast gently. "Yup, it's time to feed him, too."

Leah turned her attention back around. "It's been a pleasure, Annie. Welcome to the family. Oh, and Mom will fix something for you to eat, too. I'll see you soon."

6 What's a woman to wear?

It was a good thing that none of us were fashion conscious. We wore what we had, regardless of the latest trends. It wasn't because we were snobs, preferring to wear our traditional garb; it was just that we were pretty much destitute in the apparel area. If it was warm, at least semi-comfortable, and covered what society dictated that we should (legs from the ankles up, arms from shoulders to elbows), we wore it. All I had to share with Annie was my sleeping gown, the only spare outfit I owned. No big deal; I could go back to sleeping in my shift. I usually did that in the summer anyway. Besides, I had a reliable and easily accessible heater—my husband—to sleep next to. All Annie had was the pallet composed of our one and only spare quilt and the banked coals and retained heat at the brick hearth. Still, that bed was probably more suitable than what she'd had—in the recent past, at least.

Annie wanted to help around the house, but because her frostbitten toes limited her mobility, there really wasn't much she could do. She stayed at her station, the south-facing sunny window, weaving baskets. She seemed content in her tiny realm. Occasionally a frown would appear, but then she'd look up at her surroundings, and a sweet smile would scurry in and take its place.

Sarah and Jody had returned the day after her baptism of cleanliness. They liked her as much as the rest of us, and she was comfortable with them, too. However, now our accommodations were even more snug. We were all able to sit at the table, and had our own sleeping stations, but the children definitely had to go outside or over to James and Leah's to play. Occasionally, the wee three would gather beside Annie and share their 'picture' book with her. Her sweet smile was genuine, her gentle touch to smooth a child's hair out of his or her eyes really wasn't needed—I think she just wanted to touch something pure and possible.

I had to wonder what Jenny 'knew' about Annie becoming a mother that we didn't. She had the sight, not me, but either way, that little tidbit of ESP—or whatever they called it now—she had shared seemed to soothe Annie. Apparently, she really did want children, just not with the wrong man. Smart gal.

Today Sarah and I were making small talk about the recent trip she had made to see a former officer in the Continental Army. Colonel Holt was still as crotchety as ever, she said, but having a major flare-up of gout didn't help. I appreciated getting her version of an 18th century news update, gathered from handbills, newspapers, and gossip she had heard during her trip to the coast.

Sarah suddenly sat up straight, then leaned forward to share her inspiration with me in confidence, not that Annie was an eavesdropper.

"I have the perfect dress for Annie!" she said softly, containing her enthusiasm with clenched fists. "I had forgotten all about it until just now. It was a gift, rather a payment, from one of the ladies I attended last autumn, a chief's wife. She had broken her ankle when she was faced with the decision to either jump off a cliff or face a wounded bear. She decided she had a better chance with the rocks and trees than his long claws, sharp teeth and riled attitude, so she jumped. When I came back to check on her three weeks later, she had crafted a beautiful buckskin dress for me. It would have been an insult not to accept it, but as we all know, I'd really stand out if I wore it anywhere but here in the house. Even then, I'd have to be wary of unexpected callers seeing me essentially *déshabillé*."

Sarah was right. She had to be a bit more presentable since she was the traveling healer in this area of North Carolina, tending to Native American chiefs and children, dirt farmers and estate owners, wandering former soldiers now without a cause, and government officials on duty, far away from their private physicians. Anyone with an owie or a fever knew that she was there to help.

"Now, where did I put that?" She went to her side of the main room and pulled the wooden chest out from under her high four-poster bed. "Ah, here it is, right on top."

Annie had continued her basketwork while Sarah and I carried on. If she understood our conversation or had any idea about what we were talking about, it didn't show. Her hands continued to weave the split river cane in a never ending, or almost so, concentric plate. I had watched her earlier, mesmerized by her magic and how she seamlessly brought up the sides into a bowl shape. It had taken her almost a full day to complete the first one, but she was more than halfway done with her second basket in just hours. I don't think she had a chance to practice her skill while with 'he,' but she was making up for lost time now.

"Annie, I have a gift for you," Sarah said and knelt down beside her.

Well, it was hard to tell which was rounder: Annie's eyes or her mouth. "Pretty!" she said when she saw the embellished dress. She set her work in progress on her lap and gently touched the soft doeskin. She quickly pulled back, her mouth closed in a polite smile. "You dress pretty."

Sarah turned to me and asked, "How are her feet? Can she stand yet?"

"Oh, she can stand, but she toddles a bit. She can walk short distances, like to the dinner table or the privy, but I discourage her from helping around the house. Besides, she already told me that she's making the baskets for Leah, Jenny, and me. I think she likes the strict orders to stay off her feet so she can get more of them made. Wallace just brought her a fresh harvest of cane and Jenny donated the honeysuckle vines she collected last spring. I guess it was a good thing that we didn't get around to cleaning out the barn. The raw material for her baskets was like an early Christmas gift."

"Then let's make it two gifts. Annie, I'd like you to stand

up," Sarah told her, offering her a hand to help her to her feet.

Annie looked at me to be sure it was allowed, that she wasn't going against my wishes to stay put. "Go ahead. She wants to see if the dress fits."

She accepted the help up, but was still wary, her shoulders drooped and hands lax at her side, fingers twitching in uncertainty.

Sarah held the dress up to Annie's back, then looked down to check the length. "I don't know what the appropriate hem length is for a Cherokee woman's dress, but if it's too long, she can trim it." Sarah peeked out the window to make sure no one was on the way in.

"Coast is clear."

"Annie, reach for the sky!" I said and raised my arms high. I looked and felt like a complete idiot. "You, too," I said, and dropped one hand to pull hers up. "Both of them, come on. You need to help me. You can take off my nightgown now because you got a new dress."

And there she was again: my wide-eyed and mouth opened in shock, Annie. "Me dress?" she asked.

"If it fits," I answered. "And if it doesn't, we can do some modifications." I could tell she didn't understand my long answer. "Yes. Put it on."

Sarah finished the strip and re-dress procedure as I kept an eye out for unexpected family. Annie was barely cooperating, but I think she was still stunned. Not only a dress just for her, but a new one in the style of her heritage, too.

"I wish we had a full-length mirror so she could see herself," Sarah said as she shifted the fit across the shoulders.

"Well, I don't think Leah ever took hers back. I mean, it's just a handheld looking glass, but it's better than nothing." I reached up and retrieved it from the kids-free zone on the mantel above the fireplace. "Look, Annie. Sarah has given you this dress. Isn't it pretty?"

I held the handle and moved the mirror up and down like a wand held by a TSA security agent at an airport terminal. *Zap!* Another random 21st century memory. I shook my head to get rid of the pesky, no-good image.

"No?" Annie asked.

"Huh?"

"I think you confused her when you shook your head,

Evie." Sarah turned her attention back to Annie. "Yes, the dress is yours. It, um, won't fit me," she fibbed. She took the mirror from my flashback-dazed hand and gave it to Annie. "Look for yourself."

Annie held it in front of her chest, then lowered it, and eventually turned around in place, trying to catch up to the image. "Thank you, Sarah," she said, concentrating on saying the new name correctly. "Very pretty."

***

Annie had been with us almost a week now. Her frostbitten toes were pretty much healed. The dead skin at the tips of her big toes sloughed off, and her walking improved. She was as sure-footed as anyone else in the family now. She still didn't have any shoes or slippers, though. She made do by stepping into my boots when she needed to go outside to the privy, but that was just a temporary situation. I only had one pair of shoes, and no matter how generous I tried to be, I wasn't going to give away my one and only, especially since they didn't fit her. She had tried to weave some slippers, but that didn't work out because we had the wrong materials.

"I had good shoes," she said, pointing to her feet. "From

grass. One day, *he* say he cold, so he throw them in fire." Her face reddened as she shared the story with words and hand language. "'These for you,' he say." She pinched her nose.

"That's when he made you wear the polecat slippers?" Jenny asked.

Annie nodded, her face still red.

"I'm sorry we can't get any grass so you can make more like your old ones," Jenny said, signing and talking at the same time. "But you'll get new shoes, I know it."

I rolled my eyes and looked up at Wallace. "Whatever she says will happen, will," he said to Annie. "I'd volunteer to set a few traps, but the whole process from trap to workable leather takes time."

"And chemicals or animal organs that we don't have," I added. "Jenny's right. I'm sure Annie will get some footwear for Christmas. She's already been blessed in so many ways. What's to make us think that the Lord won't continue?"

Suddenly, Jenny started jumping up and down, then ran to the window, peering out through the frosty pane. "He's here, he's here!"

We weren't expecting anyone, and Jenny didn't get that

excited about James and Leah, so it was evident that Jenny had anticipated company.

Wallace opened the door and stepped outside, closing the door behind him. "Wait here," he called back to Jenny. He peered down the trail and saw a tall rider on a mule coming his way. He ignored the sound of Jenny's bouncing up and down, glad that Evie was telling her to hush and be patient.

A long minute later, the man Jenny had 'seen' came into our view. Wallace reached inside, grabbed his coat, said, "Wait here," than walked up to meet the traveler near the barn. "Greetings, Samuel. I see you found our house. Let's take the mule into the barn, then you can come inside and warm yourself by the fire."

Jenny moved out of the way quickly when the door opened. "Samuel! You found us! You found us! Come in and sit down. Can I get you something to drink? Ooh, ooh. I'll make you some raspberry tea."

Samuel smiled at the little blonde who was glad to see him, then looked around the room and saw someone he didn't know.

"Let me introduce you to my wife, Evie. Our three youngest children are visiting their kin," Wallace touched his fingertips together to indicate the tepee-shaped home, "and will be back later. Oh, and I'm sure you remember Annie."

Only, if only I had a camera! The look on the faces of those two was positively priceless. I swear, the air was golden with the excitement and shock and, well, maybe love was a bit premature, but it sure felt like that to me!

Wallace stepped up to Samuel and put a hand on his shoulder. "You two never did get a proper introduction, did you? Annie, this is Samuel. Samuel, this is our friend Annie."

Those two didn't look alike except for their coloring, but their expressions were identical. And their transitions from shock to absolute pleasure blossomed at the same rate, too. Looked like Annie was going to be a Mrs. Samuel soon.

"So, what brings you to this area of the woods, Samuel?" Wallace asked, although it was obvious why he was had made the long trip: Annie.

Samuel's head shook as he came back from the world of Annie to the world of everything else. "Shoes. I bring shoes for Annie." He brought out a rawhide-tied parcel, then set it on the table.

"Come on over and see what he brought you, Annie," I said, and walked with her to the table, holding on to her elbow. She was a bit shaky on her feet, but it didn't have anything to do with the frostbit toes or pain. She was in I-can't-believe-my-dream-has-come-true land, for sure.

Jenny felt the excitement, too, but still managed to make a cup of tea for Samuel. "Here you are," she said, breaking his trance. "We don't have honey," and handed the starry-eyed man the crude baked-clay mug she had made last summer, "but it still tastes good. Can you stay for dinner?"

Jenny suddenly realized that it wasn't her place to invite company to eat at her parent's home. "I mean…" She looked up to her father with a mixture of 'I'm sorry' and 'Can he stay, please?'

"Yes, Samuel, we'd be pleased to have you stay for our evening meal. It's a long ride back. We don't have room in here, but it isn't too cold in the barn with all those goats inside."

I could tell that Samuel was trying not to smile, wanting to keep a stoic non-committal demeanor, but it wasn't working. He looked over at Annie and gave in to the smile, but still held back the giddiness we all knew he felt. "Thank you. That would be good. Mule is tired."

"And you are, too, huh?" Jenny asked.

"Jenny!" Wallace and I shouted at the same time.

She looked at us and said, "But he is, isn't he? It was a long ride. And maybe he got lost once or twice, but he's here now. I'll go to the cellar and get some more potatoes and cornmeal. I know it's not Thanksgiving, but we can still celebrate!"

***

I'm not sure which excited Jenny more: having the spontaneous Thanksgiving meal or being able to use her new Morse paging system to call James, Leah, and family to the house.

"Why all the clangs, Jenny?" James asked as he stepped in the door.

Jenny looked behind him. "Where's everyone else? I clanged it six times, then added another three for River. I didn't think you'd want to leave him behind. 'Sides, he's invited to dinner, too. He likes smashed potatoes, even though he'd rather squish them than eat them."

James had been looking around the room, trying to get a direct answer without Jenny's dissertation on bells and baby food. I saw his confusion segue into an 'aha' moment.

"Yes, we have company for dinner tonight, James," I

said. "This is Samuel. Jenny and Wallace met him the last time they went to town. You're all invited to eat with us, but I think you'd better go back and give Leah a hand in getting the two little ones over rather than pulling the paging rope a few more times. I hope she hasn't already fixed dinner."

"Nice to meet you, Samuel." James nodded in greeting, then took the shy man's hand and shook it, placing his other on top, letting him know he was genuinely glad to meet him.

"It's just chili," he said. "It'll taste better after cooking an extra day, anyway. I'll be right back. Jenny, if it's all right with your mother, would you come give me a hand?"

"Go ahead," I told Jenny, then mouthed 'thank you' to James.

Jenny's face fell into a frown. She wanted to stay with Samuel and Annie. She knew she wasn't supposed to tell Samuel and Annie things 'she knew' about them and their future, but just being next to this happy 'future' couple made her feel giddy and tingly inside, too.

***

Jody and Sarah were back on the road again, and it was a good thing. There was barely enough room at the dinner table for all the adults, but we managed. Jenny sat with

80

Judah, Leo, Wren, and Bibby Liz, eating her meal with River trapped under her left arm, feeding him bits of mashed potatoes. She'd look up from her catering duty and gaze at the shy young couple, visualizing them as a happily married couple with a baby, then frown as an alternate future tried to sneak in.

Waaa!

"Sorry about that, River," she said and fed him another bit. "I get distracted sometimes."

It was no accident that I put Annie and Samuel right next to each other and across from me. I guess I was a romantic at heart, and since I didn't have any chick flicks or romance novels, watching a real-life love affair bloom right before my eyes was a real treat.

"Cornbread, please," Wallace asked, nudging my arm.

"Oh, sorry," I replied, and handed him the plate of sourdough cornbread muffins.

"You know, I only bumped you to get your attention," he whispered in my ear. "I asked you three times. You'd better stop staring. Not that they'd notice…"

We both looked at the couple and saw they were still head down, smiling, as they ate their dinner. I was tempted to drop my napkin on the floor to look under the table to see if they were holding hands, but that would have been rude and probably an invasion of their privacy. No, definitely a violation of both privacy and courtesy.

"Samuel, in our culture, we celebrate the birth of our savior, Jesus Christ, every year on December 25th. We decorate a tree, maybe exchange handmade or inexpensive gifts, sing songs, and read the story of His birth in the Bible. We'd be happy to have you join us."

Samuel looked toward the door, the glow he had moments earlier now gone.

"Oh, I'm sorry. I'm sure you don't use our calendar. Two days after the next new moon. At least, that's what we call it: when no light comes from the moon. Two days after that is our celebration. Please join us. I know Jenny and Annie want you to come back soon."

"I would like that. If the weather allows, I will come. Much easier now because I have mule," he said, his eyes shining with pride.

7 Bedding in the barn

"You should be comfortable in here with the animals. If we had more floorspace available, I'd ask you to stay inside with the rest of us. As it is, we've slept head to toe many nights. Our plans for a home separate from my parents keeps getting postponed. At least, James and Leah have their own residence now, even if it isn't completed," Wallace said, then realized he was probably losing Samuel in his expanded discussion on why he had asked him to sleep in the barn for the night.

"I see you have a blanket," he said, continuing his tour with hand gestures. "Jenny and I changed out the straw," pointing to the hay, "just this morning, so at least it smells fresh in here," and sniffed. "I'm sorry I don't have another lantern to share," and held up the windproof oil light. "The children broke our second one and I haven't had a chance to replace it," pretending to drop it.

"At least you'll be protected from the wind." Wallace stepped out of the doorway and looked up into the dark sky, assessing the moist breeze as it blew across and chilled his bare face. "And from the snow." He motioned snow falling by waving his fingers. "I think we'll have snowfall by morning."

"This is good," Samuel said. He looked around the small barn with the caged chickens and two pens, one with four goats corralled, the other filled with the fresh straw that had been raked into a low mound, perfect for bedding. "Thank you."

"Now, don't leave without coming in for breakfast. I'm sure Annie would like to see you again before you leave."

"Yes. I will see you and your family before I leave," he said, then unintentionally sighed, "And Annie."

***

"So, do you think it's going to snow tonight?" I asked when Wallace came back in.

"If it does, it might give Samuel an excuse to stay another day." He peeked over the privacy curtain at Annie to see if she had heard him. She must have, he thought, because she was snuggling into her quilt, smiling.

"I may not remember Leah as a teenager with a crush on a boy," I whispered to Wallace as he slipped into bed with me, "but I'd say Annie was at risk of sneaking out to see

Samuel tonight."

"I don't know the word crush, but if it means she's infatuated with the man, I agree."

"Well, they're both adults. Besides, Indian culture is different than ours. It might be perfectly acceptable for them to…um…form a union without courting, an engagement, a wedding…"

I suddenly became excited with the thought of a young couple, enjoying those first powerful flushes of 'infatuation.' "I think the babies are all asleep. How about pretending you and I are together for the first time?"

Wallace snuggled under my chin, kissing my neck softly as he worked his way up to my eager mouth. He took his time, his soft and almost lackadaisical kisses driving me nuts! Finally, I tapped his shoulder, letting him know to turn up the heat.

He pulled away and whispered, "I didn't know much our first time. How about if we pretend it was the next week, when I found all your *erogenous* zones," he whispered, purring the one word, then slipped a warm hand on my fanny, gently tugging up my shift.

I squirmed up, down, and around, helping him pull my

shift off over my head, then lay back and giggled softly. "Just like the tenth time," I whispered. "I'll never forget that one!"

***

Annie could tell by the whispers and giggles that Wallace and Evie were joining. She knew 'how' to do it but had never enjoyed it. Now she knew what was wrong, though. It had to be with the right man. She had seen three happy couples in the short time she'd been here: Wallace and Evie, James and Leah, and very briefly, Sarah and Jody. Maybe there was something spiritual about this part of the mountain. If so, she should visit Samuel in the barn and see if he wanted to be the fourth couple.

She burrowed deeper into the quilt. Even if this place wasn't sacred or spiritual, she still wanted to be with him. He couldn't come to her, though. There wasn't enough room for another person to lie down in this house unless he was lying on top of her.

The thought sent warm shivers and tingles to her lady parts. That must be what the other women in the tribe told her was the way to find out if a man was right for her or not. She thought of Samuel at dinner, telling Wallace that he'd come back to see her and Jenny two days after the moon went dark. Another wave of warmth flooded her nether regions. She'd go see him tonight, before he left, just in case he didn't make it back again. She looked up at the window. The moon was full. and even with the clouds, there was plenty of light to see the way.

Annie slipped on her new moccasins, then wrapped the quilt around her shoulders, stepping softly to the door. The little pants and giggles coming from Wallace and Evie's side of the curtain would cover any noises she made opening and shutting the heavy door. She lifted the wooden latch and let herself out, easing the rod into the carved channel so it didn't even scrape.

She sniffed the air. Snow was coming. She'd better hurry to the barn while the ground was still dry.

***

Samuel lay on the straw, his blanket covering him up to his chest. He moved his hand over the front of his breechclout and rearranged himself. He couldn't stop thinking about Annie, about how much he wanted her for his wife, and those thoughts had aroused his man parts. Maybe he should have remarried soon after his first wife died in childbirth, but now all the available women had either married outside of the village or had died of the measles. Even his mother was eager for him to bring Annie back. As soon as he told her about the polecat moccasins and how a white family had 'adopted' her, she told him that she would make a pair of marriage slippers for the woman. Go to her. If she accepted them, then she would be his.

His thoughts were interrupted by a scratching at the barn door. Something, or someone, was trying to get in. He rolled off the straw pallet and listened for the sound of a wild animal.

The soft grunts were human, a female trying to lift the door latch that had swollen from the moisture in the air. He tapped his side of the bar with the side of his fist and the door swung open. "Come inside," he said, glad that he could speak Cherokee again. He nodded to the bed of straw. "It's still warm."

Annie thought about bringing the quilt she had wrapped around her shoulders to his bed, then changed her mind, and instead folded it and set it on the milking stool. She didn't want to get it covered in straw. That would be a sure sign that she'd been out to see Samuel.

While her back was to him, Samuel got under the

blanket. He untied his breechclout, but let it stay in place. He wasn't a virgin and knew it would be easier to join with her if he didn't have clothing in the way.

"Do you like the moccasins?" he asked. She turned toward him and he motioned to her, asking her to come under the blanket with him.

Annie removed her fancy footwear and set them down near the bed. "They're beautiful. Did you make them?"

"No, my mother did. She said I was to give them to the woman I wanted to marry."

"Oh," Annie said sadly, thinking that she might have to give them back, then realized that he had given them to her for that very purpose. "Oh!"

"You might be more comfortable sleeping with me tonight if you took off your dress," he said, not even trying to hide his smile of anticipation.

Annie chuckled. "Then you, too. Here, hand me your clothing and I'll set them here. But hurry. It's cold!"

Samuel stared wide-eyed at her firm nipples, eager to make them warm with his mouth. He blinked as he pulled his shirt off over his head, keeping the image in his mind, then shimmied out of his breechclout, glad that he had already removed his leggings and moccasins.

Annie quickly folded his clothes and set them on top of hers, then scurried under the blanket. "You're so warm," she said, her hands held together under her chin.

"You'd receive more body warmth if you wrapped your arms around me."

Annie loosened her grip. "Please, make me warm all over. And I'll warm you, too."

***

The chickens rustling in their cage roused Samuel and Annie at the same time. "Good morning, wife."

Annie giggled, then rubbed up against the part of him that had made her his wife. "Good morning, husband." She squinted at the crack above the door frame. "It's nearly daylight. I should return before they see I came to you."

"No. Stay here." He ran his hand down the curve of her back, caressing her round bottom, then pulled her closer to him. "I'm sure Wallace knows where you are. If Evie hasn't figured it out, he'll tell her. And they'll both keep Jenny from coming out here. No. We'll stay for more of what the White Man calls lovemaking, then I'll go in the house with you. I will tell them you are coming with me, as my wife, to my village."

"Your wife," Annie said, the warmth of those words adding to the warmth of her woman parts. "Yes. I like lovemaking." She giggled. "I like the word *and* the act." She grabbed him by his happy husband tool. "Again."

***

It was no surprise that Annie wasn't at her sleeping station in front of the hearth when we got up. Jenny and the wee three were still abed, snuggled together against the chill. Wallace added more wood to the smoldering coals and awakened the fire while I poured more water into the kettle. We both smiled, not just because we knew what had happened, but because it had instigated one of the most passionate nights we'd been able to share with one another in ages. Maybe we had made a baby—or two, if what Leah said was right. I sure hoped so.

I was in the middle of feeding porridge with dried blueberries to my family when Samuel and Annie finally came in.

"There they are!" Jenny exclaimed. "I didn't say anything, but I knew you didn't run off in the middle of the night."

"Good morning, you two," I said. "I hope it wasn't too cold out there last night."

"Here, enjoy some hot tea," Wallace said, then offered the two mugs he had prepared for us to them.

The two accepted, visibly capturing the heat of the earthenware cups with their hands, their noses red with cold.

"Come sit with me, Annie," Jenny called. "You sure look extra pretty this morning."

"Yes, she does," Samuel said. "She is my wife now." He turned to Wallace. "I thank you and your family for all you have done for me and my wife. My tribe had…"

"Hard times? Wallace suggested. "No food, too much sickness? That's hard times."

"Yes, we had hard times, but now we have much food and meat. I make a shelter for my wife, too. She can ride mule back to my village. I have big bear skin to keep her warm, too."

"You'll still come see us at Christmas, won't you?" asked Jenny, "Both of you?"

Annie put her hand on Samuel's arm, silently imploring him to grant Jenny's—and probably hers, too—request.

He looked down at his wife, then over at Jenny, her eyes shiny with unspilled tears. "If the weather is good, we will come. Two days after the new moon."

"Congratulations to both of you," I said. "I kinda, sorta thought you might be leaving together, so I put aside some food for your trip. It isn't much, just dried apples and some corn muffins. Let's eat some breakfast, and then you can decide what you need to take from here for your new life as Mrs. Samuel."

I didn't know if the Cherokee used last names or not, and I'm certain that Annie didn't understand everything I said, but I could tell by the way she watched what I said and smiled at certain remarks, like 'Mrs. Samuel,' that she had the meat of my meaning.

The two of them politely ate their fruit-sweetened oatmeal, then Samuel nodded to Annie, then looked toward the corner that had been her bedroom/crafting area.

"Excuse me," she said, having learned good old-fashioned table manners from me as I was teaching them to my youngest three. She stood tall as she walked to the corner, her bearing so much different than it had been when she was a single woman. She knelt to the floor and gathered all the basket materials, placing the coils of split reed and stripped honeysuckle vine neatly in the largest basket. The other baskets were already nested, stowed beside the cupboard. She placed these on top of the weaving products, then brought the bounty to me.

"This one is for you," she said, and handed me largest basket. "Jenny can weave now, but she must ask you when is good time. She has other chores, too."

"Please give this one to Leah, the healer." The second largest basket had a woven ribbon attached to the side, something I'd never seen in baskets in this day and age.

"For Granny. I only saw her one day, but she's good woman for this family and gave me my dress."

The basket was just a bit smaller than the other two, but I think that was just so they'd nest. I didn't know she had made this many. I did remember seeing her make the smallest one, though.

"This is for Jenny," she said and handed her a basket about five inches long and three inches wide and tall. What made this one so special was that it had a lid and small clasp on the front of it, like a treasure or keepsake box. "For summer when you gather your pretty rocks by the water. Keep them here."

"All right," Jenny sniffed as she accepted the gift. "You remember to come see us for Christmas." She held up ten fingers, closed her hands, then added four more. "I *know* we'll have something special for you."

Annie nodded to Wallace, then me, and said, "Thank you for saving me. And for being my friend." She turned to Jenny and rubbed her nose on Jenny's cheek. "You are special. I no need gift. I have you and family for friends."

Well, the men shook hands, the kids came over and hugged Annie's legs, asking why she was leaving, did they do something wrong; you know, the usual farewell mayhem. They had finally made it out the door, when I remembered that I hadn't given them their' on the road' food parcel.

"Here, you stay inside with the children or Samuel and Annie will never be able to leave. I'll take this to them," Wallace said, and grabbed the twined-wrapped package.

Samuel was adjusting the bear skin over Annie when Wallace caught up with them. "That's a big pelt. I don't think I've ever seen a black bear hide that big." Wallace looked it over, admiring the stitching at the edges, when he saw the patched area.

"It looks like this bear was shot with buckshot."

"This is man-killer bear. It killed two men and chased down wife of chief from other tribe. She can walk now.

Granny fix her leg. Now bear keep this chief's wife warm."

"Oh, so you're a chief? I should have guessed. You are an honorable man. I'm proud that Annie is your wife now. Be safe on your trip home." Wallace looked up at the sky. "Good weather for you."

"See you in," Samuel put up his hands to indicate thirteen, "days. We come one day sooner to surprise your Jenny."

"You do that. I'm sure we'd all appreciate having guests for an extra day."

8 Faith

Someone or something was frantically kicking at our door. It was the middle of the night and I wasn't going to answer it. That's what I had a husband for. Or one of the reasons I had a husband.

Wallace grabbed a poker iron with one hand and pushed up the latch on the door with the other. We didn't have a lock, but did have a thick lath across the door just in case a wild critter smelled food inside and decided to come in uninvited.

I heard the contorted noise even before the door was opened. It was human. And the human was in pain, severe emotional pain.

"Wee Ian," I whispered hoarsely, "I mean, Scout. What are you doing out at this time of night and what's that?"

The son of my first husband, Wee Ian Kincaid—or Scout as he had been renamed by my daughter Jenny—was at the door with a wad of cloth held close to his chest. Tears streaked his dirty adolescent face. It looked as if he had been crying for hours by the redness of his eyes. "What's wrong," I

97

asked, presenting him with a new question since he hadn't answered my first two.

"Can ye help her?" he asked, then thrust his rag-wrapped bundle at me.

I unwrapped the first layer of coarse feed bag and gasped. It was a baby, still alive, but by the rapid, shallow breathing, not for long. "Who…what…why…" I babbled.

"Can ye, will ye, please?" he begged.

I didn't bother asking for the history: the child needed fluids immediately. "Jenny, do we still have that bottle around here we used for Bibby Liz?"

Jenny was wiping her eyes and blinking them rapidly, trying to work the sleep out of them. "Um, I think so." She turned upside down and looked under her bed. "Oh yeah," she said in embarrassment, "here it is."

"Why, what? Never mind. Would you put some water on to boil and put the bottle, cap, and nipple in it, too? Wallace, go get me some milk out of the spring house. I only need about half a cup, probably less, but half a cup will be good for a start. Jenny, after you get the fire going, get the spare metal dipper and make sure it's clean. I need you to put the cup end of it into the boiling water, too, but only for a minute."

I looked up and saw Scout sniffling, still scared beyond his tender years with the responsibility he had just transferred to me. I gave him a weak smile, then a nod for him to join me in prayer. "Okay, Lord, you've kept this baby alive this far, I'm sure you didn't mean for him or her to die now. Please give the child all the strength needed and…um…maybe a little extra. Oh, and some wisdom for me, too, so I'll know what to do. In Jesus's name, amen."

I sighed, then pulled the cloth back again to make sure the child was still breathing, then urged it down a little more to do a quick gender check. "Well, Scout, from what I recall, girls are inherently stronger than boys, so she already has a better chance of survival. Come sit next to me and tell me what happened."

I sat down on the edge of the bed and dipped my pinkie into the water cup on my little night table. I put my damp digit into her mouth, trying to see if she had the instinct to suck. Her face moved almost imperceptibly as she checked out the *faux* nipple. Her mouth opened but didn't close. She was too weak to pull her little purple tongue back in, but I could almost swear that she sneered at the deception. "Hang in there, sweetie, we have some real milk coming soon."

Scout was still mum, but I doubt it was because he didn't want to interrupt me while I was talking to the baby. He was in shock. Or scared wordless. Or totally terrified. Or all three. Well, I wasn't in a nosy mood right now, and he and the baby were both breathing. I had something more important on my mind—I had to remember how to make formula.

Wallace and Jenny were taking care of sterilizing the lone bottle, cap, and nipple and the dipper. "Didn't you use sugar in Bibby's formula?" Wallace asked.

"Oh, shoot, I'm glad you remembered. We still have a little left, I'm sure. I can't use honey to sweeten the milk because the bacteria in it are bad for an infant's digestive tract..." I looked at my nightshirt-clad family and the scruffy adolescent savior and added, "I just have to make sure we use sugar until her belly's older."

The three of them made an 'aha' expression, then breathed a sigh of relief. I knew Wallace was aware of my 21st century knowledge when it came to science, but it looked as if Scout and Jenny were also onto me now. Oh well, I could only hope they knew. Now I wouldn't have to find a way to tell them. Either way, they trusted my judgment as the mother of the house. I was the authority on babies, at least until Sarah or Leah came in, and then we shared the mentor's mantle.

"Wallace, put the milk in the dipper and hold it over the fire to get it to scald, just so it gets a little film over the top of it. Oh, and Jenny, sterilize the spoon, too. That means…" I saw her all-knowing grin again. "You know what sterilizing is, don't you?"

"Brother James taught me. Besides, I helped my sister, Leah, sterilize the bottles for Bibby Liz. You want to make sure there aren't any germs on the spoon when you stir in the sugar, huh? And that all the germs are killed in the milk, too."

"Yes, but heating also breaks down the proteins so they're easier for a baby to digest. Mother's milk would be best for her, but I'm all dried up. If she can tolerate this and get through the next couple of days, heck, if she gets through the night, she'll be fine, I'm sure."

"I hope so," Scout said sadly, softly uttering his first words since his panicked request for help at the door.

I looked over at Wallace and saw he had a peaceful smile on his face, one that I remembered from somewhere… Oh yeah! He had that same look of contentment when he helped bring my youngest daughter into the world. With the parental status of this wee little girl unknown, I think he's hoping that we had just painlessly delivered another daughter.

He wasn't the biological father of any of my children but claimed them just the same. Wren, Leo, and Judah were a lot smaller than this one when they were born. This one was smaller than Leah's babies had been, but she still had some chubbiness to her. If she was premature, it wasn't by more than a couple weeks. Hopefully, this new delivery would be as strong as Wren, my smallest.

Jenny knew the bottle drill and used a pair of wooden tongs to pull the bottle out of the water, making sure all the water was out before she set it on a folded cloth. She repeated the procedure for the cap and nipple. James was so sly, bringing them along in his 'science' kit from the 21st century. Leah had been insulted when she found out about them, believing that he didn't think she would be able to nurse a baby. He said he had honestly forgotten about it until they needed it. Well, I believed him. If he had thought about it, Leah would have read his mind and known about it, too. Regardless, when she found out she was pregnant with her second child and wouldn't be able to nurse wee Bibby Liz at the same time, that bottle was a Godsend. Or blessing. Or whatever. And now it was going to be put to good use again.

"I just adjusted the formula for this small amount. I verified my computations with Jenny," Wallace said, and winked at her. She was sharp with math and just about all her other school work. She still needed some work with spelling, but at least she wrote the words phonetically so I could figure them out. She'd be a perfect student if she had a computer with spell check.

"It is okay if I cool down the bottle in a pan of cold water, isn't it?" Wallace asked.

"Yes, as long as the nipple isn't on it yet. I want to get some formula in her as soon as possible. If you haven't already filled it, only put about an inch in there. It'll cool faster and I doubt she can handle much more than that. I think this is her first food."

I looked down at Scout, still stunned at whatever it was that had brought him to our threshold. "She's never eaten before, has she?" I asked softly.

He shook his head. "Her mother, my stepmother, was deid when I...I...I birthed her. I could see Raven's belly movin' after her heart and breathin' stopped. I had to do *somethin'!* I remembered when you did the surgery on the goat, Sarah P. I...I ken how ye felt, but this time I couldna help the mother, only the bairn. I feel bad because I had to leave Raven's body there. I couldna take the time to bury her and still get the bairn to ye. There wasna anyone any closer, or at least anyone I trusted to ken what to do fer her.

"I dinna ken if my da was coming back soon or not, but I kent someone would be by eventually lookin' fer him. He managed to make some men mad at him again. I think they're the ones who did that to Raven—kilt her. She was alive when I got there. She kept tellin' me to take care of my little brother. She didna ken she was havin' a daughter. She wanted a son to make Da happy. But nothin' would make him happy." Scout shook his head. "And now he's gonna be madder still. It willna bring her back or help the wee'un, either. Maybe Wallace and I can go back in the mornin' and bury her. That is, if ye can watch the bairn. Would ye want another daughter? I dinna care to let my Da ken he had a daughter. I'd rather he thought that Raven and the baby died together. If we bury her, he'll never ken what she died of unless her killers tell him..." Scout's tone suddenly changed to anger, "because I sure willna tell him! There's too much hate and revenge in his life. He doesna need to have a reason for more."

Wallace had filled the bottle and brought it to me as Scout related his story. I checked the temperature on the inside of my wrist. "Perfect," I said, then touched the nipple to her cheek. Her eyes fluttered but didn't open. I touched it to her lips, but she didn't seem interested.

"Okay, here," I said and dripped a drop on my pinkie. "Now, this isn't water this time, little lady."

Still nothing.

"Okay, I think I know what you need." I snuggled her up to my chest, as if I was going to nurse her, and blew in her face. "Now, I'm your new mommy, and you have to eat so you can get big and strong and play with all of your brothers and sisters. *Manga!*" I commanded and brushed my milky pinkie on her bottom lip.

"Well, I'll be," Wallace said, as she opened her mouth. "You're listening to Mommy already. That's a good little girl."

The baby dipped her head and put her mouth on my finger and exerted a very faint but definite suction. I quickly swapped my finger for the nipple and let her try. Her mouth stopped. She didn't like the polymer prosthetic. "Okay, you win for now." I dripped more formula on my pinkie and trickled it into her mouth, allowing her to give a weak sucking motion to accomplish the needed swallowing.

After half a dozen small drops, she was done. She closed her eyes and panted erratically. I knew the effort had exhausted her already weak body. Hopefully, she'd only nap for a short time, then wake for a few more drops.

I looked up at my rapt audience. Wallace was still beaming. "Scout, you need to go to sleep, too. Lie down over there on Jenny's bed with her," he said, gently patting the tired boy on the shoulder, urging him to lie down on the bed rather than stay in his current upright and wavering position. "You'll both fit. I'm sure you want to be in the same room as your sister."

"Aye, I could do with a nap, but ye have it wrong, Wallace. She's my kin, my father's cousin's daughter, not my sister. And I ken a little of the Bible," he said with pride. "I have faith that she'll live until tomorrow, at least."

"Well, Scout, I agree with you to an extent. My youngest daughter, Faith, will live, but I'm sure it will be much longer than just until tomorrow. You see, I think tomorrow is already here—it's after midnight. Now, get some rest. Cuddle up to

Jenny, and I'm sure you'll be slumbering soon."

A smile crept up the side of Scout's mouth, making its way toward his ear. "Aye, I'd appreciate some rest and comfort. It's been a long day and a half."

***

I settled into my nursing chair with Faith wrapped in one of my babies' old receiving blankets, a napkin folded up as a clout between her red, bowed legs. I doubt she had enough fluid in her to make a mess, but she might as well get used to diapers now. Besides, I knew that sometime in the first 48 hours, she'd have a bowel movement even if she hadn't nursed. I didn't want to ask if it had happened yet or not. Scout was already sound asleep, Jenny's arm wrapped around his waist, the smile of contentment on his face surpassed only by the one on hers.

I nudged the bottle's nipple to the side of her mouth, hoping she'd follow its pressure and latch on by herself. She did! I was so excited that I swear I felt the milk tingling in my own breasts even though I hadn't nursed a baby in ages. Well, after I made sure little missy was going to be strong enough, I'd let her try out my natural nipple. Of course, I'd do it on the sly. Sarah had told me about Jane, the virgin wet nurse. She had never had a baby yet was able to put both wee Julian and Bibby to her breast and nurse them. Evidently the stimulation that her randy fiancé Benji had provided earlier had kicked in her lactating hormones.

If I could get her to stimulate mine, we wouldn't have to mess with sterilizing the bottle and mixing formula. And if nursing was going to stop me from getting pregnant… Oh, well. Wallace and I had been trying for over two years and nothing had worked. Well, if he couldn't give me a baby, God could. Little Faith's black hair would be a sharp contrast to blond Jenny and the wee three's red hair, but that just meant that with my brunette Leah, I'd have the full range of hair colors. And by the earlier look of contentment on Wallace's face, he didn't care if he got a ready-made child or had to wait nine months for a build-your-own. We had one more in the family and he couldn't be happier.

9 Faux ham and friends

The days before Christmas were filled with hustle and bustle and evergreen boughs. We had a bit more room since Annie had 'eloped,' but now we had Scout. I didn't mind him sleeping with Jenny that first night, but they were both getting older and I didn't want to encourage any curiosity. Scout took over Annie's old spot at the hearth, but I think he liked that. When I got up to give Faith her bottle in the middle of the night, he stayed still—never uttered a sound or shifted position—but I knew he was awake. I could actually feel his gratitude. It was as tangible as the smell of a Damask rose: not seen, but definitely in the air and appreciated.

I had tried to nurse Faith a couple of times, hoping I'd get milk from the stimulation, but the little girl liked the bottle better. Leah admitted to me that she had tried to nurse her, too. She had milk, so that wasn't the issue. I think Faith just liked that firm silicone nipple and sweetened goat's milk. Besides, the formula helped her sleep longer. She was getting plenty of nutrition and sleeping for four hours at a time worked well for my schedule.

The younger children were intrigued by her two-inch-long, thick hair. "River didn't have hair when he was born. Is it because he's a boy and only girls get hair?" asked Wren.

"No, all of you were pretty much bald, just pink fuzz for you and your brothers, and Bibby Liz, River and even their mother, Leah, had just a hint of dark hair, not even enough to brush. I don't know about Jenny, but she was probably bald, too."

"I'm sure glad I have hair now," Wren said. "I almost have enough for braids like Jenny!"

***

Christmas day was getting closer. We all hoped that we would have meat for our Christmas dinner, but it looked like we were going to have a vegetarian menu. Our last ham had been supper for a family of mice. The cat Scout had given Jenny a couple years ago was either too full of vermin from the barn or was just plain lazy. Roast fowl was out of the question, too. There were few domesticated geese or turkeys in the New World, at least in our neighborhood, so my alternate plan to traditional fare was to have chicken. Unfortunately, that was on a fox's menu, too. We were down to three hens and a rooster. Eating our breeding stock was not an option.

"I know, I know!" Jenny exclaimed, her excited bouncy manner still more the norm than an exception. Puberty wasn't slowing her down.

"You know what, dear?"

"I can make a fox ham. That is the word, right?"

I paused, trying to figure out what in the world she was talking about, and then it hit me. "F-a-u-x is pronounced foe. And how can you make a *faux* ham?"

"We still have lots of bacon grease in the crock, and loads of potatoes, bread, a couple of eggs and I only need one beet for this. Oh, and some pie crust, but that's easy to make."

We had two days to go before Christmas, so I figured I'd let her experiment. "But this is also going to be a lesson in using scientific methods. You have your hypothesis which is can you make a *faux* ham out of what we have here. You need to write down all the ingredients, how much of each one, and how to prepare the items and in what order. That's called a recipe, by the way. Women and men have been recording recipes for…for…as long as there's been writing."

Jenny rolled her eyes at me, a new gesture I know she got from her older sister Leah.

"Okay, I'll tell you why," I said, ignoring the fact that she hadn't voiced her 'why?' "If it turns out great, you want to be able to make it again, right? And if it's a bust, you want to find out what you did wrong and not make the same mistake twice. Or three or four more times, right?"

"Right. I'll go get what I need, including the notebook James made for me, and I'll be right back."

Two hours later, Jenny's creation was complete. She allowed me to make the pie crust, but she did the rest. I hadn't thought it would turn out so well or I wouldn't have fixed a big pot of peas for supper.

"I'll tell you what, Jenny. Since I didn't have any ham to put in the peas, and I think your *faux* ham will disintegrate in the soup, how about if we just let everyone have a small piece as an *hors d'oeuvres?*"

"Huh?"

"Samples, appetizers. We'll let the family know what it tastes like tonight and tomorrow we'll have it for a main meal along with some turnips and baked apples."

"All right. And if they like it, I can make it again and again because I have the recipe!"

***

"Where did you get the ham?" Wallace asked when he came in from chopping wood. "It smells delicious. I thought we were having peas."

"Your little genius daughter… Oops! Sorry, I forgot: no labels. Our sweet Jenny came up with the idea all by herself. It's essentially a meatloaf without the meat. Mashed potatoes, a beet, bread crumbs, a couple of eggs, and some bacon grease all mixed together then wrapped in a pie crust which becomes the rind of the *faux* ham. It sure looks and smells like the real deal. Pretty clever, eh?"

"Ham! Ham! We got meat!" Judah and Leo shouted as they burst through the door.

Wren followed her brothers in. "We don't have meat because of the fox and the mice and oh, my! We got meat!"

Jenny's chest was so puffed out in pride, I thought she was going to pop her buttons. She brought it down a notch and stood in front of her culinary creation. "This is for tomorrow night 'cause we're going to have peas tonight."

"Ah, peas again?" Leo carped.

"Yeah, peas again?" Judah echoed.

113

Wren didn't say a word, but her frown of displeasure made her opinion about dinner loud and clear.

"Don't worry," Jenny said. "I'll let everyone have a hot turd before dinner."

"That's *hors d'oeuvres,* not hot turd. There's a world of difference, believe me. Now, children, wash up for dinner. I'll let Jenny slice off one piece of her ham from the end so you can tell if it tastes as good as it smells." I turned to Jenny. "That's part of the science, too."

"The proof is in the pudding," Wallace added. "It not only smells great, but it's beautiful, too. What's that round bit in the center? It looks like a bone, but I know it isn't."

Jenny giggled behind her hands. "That's just the mashed potatoes, eggs, and bread crumbs without the beet for coloring. At least we won't have to worry about nicking the knife on that bone!"

***

The faux ham hors d'oeuvres were a hit. The younger children wouldn't eat their peas until I told them that if they didn't eat their dinner tonight, they wouldn't get any of Jenny's creation tomorrow. The boys grumbled and Wren snorted, but they finished their supper.

"Do we have to go to bed? Can't we stay up for Sandy Claws?" Leo asked.

"Yeah, can we wait for Sandy Claws?" Judah echoed.

"I told you, tomorrow isn't Christmas," Wren said, her arms folded in front of her chest. Suddenly they dropped to her sides. "It isn't Christmas tomorrow, is it?"

"First off, it's Santa Claus, not sandy claws. That's what a cat gets when it walks down to the creek."

I could tell by their frowns that either they didn't get the joke or they weren't in the mood. I tried again.

"Wren's correct. Tomorrow is Christmas Eve. We'll bake some rolls, maybe another pie or three, and string some popcorn and bog berries together to hang over the boughs. James, Leah, Bibby Liz, and River will be here to help with the decorating. Later, we'll have a big meal, including Jenny's *faux* ham and turnips, read from the Bible, sing a few songs, tell each other what we're grateful for, and then, well, I guess that's about it. It's sort of like Sunday dinners, but with more singing and decorations."

"What about the presents and *Santa Claus*," Judah asked, making sure he said the name correctly.

"Well, Santa Claus and gifts don't always arrive, but

that's not what Christmas is about. Christmas is a feeling, an invisible spirit that comes from within, but it's warm and comforting like...like a daddy hug."

I saw the blank stares and realized I needed to elaborate. Again.

"You know how you feel when you've helped someone and they didn't expect it? And they were so grateful..." *They were still lost.* "Even if they forgot to say thank you, you saw it in their eyes and felt it in your bosom, right?"

Jenny started giggling at the word. I shook my head, 'not now,' and she sobered up. Well, after one uncontained chortle, she did.

"Can you imagine how the world would be if each day, one person performed a random act of kindness for no reason."

"What's random?"

"That means for no logical reason, they weren't obligated. They weren't asked to do it, it wasn't part of their jobs, and it wasn't family or kin who was in need. You know, because it was just a kind thing to do, a good deed."

"Oh, I know! I know!" Jenny popped up. "Like when we helped Annie get all pretty and clean again and let her stay here until Samuel could come ask her to be his wife. She wasn't family, and Daddy and I didn't know her when we saw her at Mr. Gibson's store, but Daddy made sure she was safe and got away from that mean old man, *he,* even though he wouldn't let her come with us until he got money."

"And we did it because we wanted to. We took care of her because that's what people are supposed to do. Do you think Jesus would want her to stay with that horrid man?"

"Nooo!" the children chorused.

"Well, Jesus is the One who told us how to treat everyone. And we celebrate His birthday on December 25th, Christmas."

"One other time I helped someone and he wasn't family or kin and he wasn't even in a bad *tickerment* like Annie."

"You mean predicament?" Wallace asked. He took off his boots by the door, hung up his coat, and settled in next to the hearth. "Do you mind if I join in the conversation? Come over here and sit next to me, children. It's cold out there and you're all so warm! Go ahead with your story, Jenny."

"You know Mr. Flynn? He's kinda crotchety sometimes, but I know he isn't mean. He's got rheumatism in his back, and I know it hurts him. But anyhow, he was trying to get rid of a big tree branch that got broke by the wind and was ready to fall onto his house. He had a saw—and it was plenty sharp—but he wasn't tall enough to get to it all the way. He was reaching up like this," Jenny illustrated an overhead sawing motion, "but he couldn't get the blade started, so I asked him if I could help.

"Well, he kinda growled, said something about how I was just a girl, but I told him I was a strong girl and I could climb a tree, even in a skirt. I don't think he believed me. He just kinda snorted and went back to swingin' that saw up in the air, tryin' to hit the branch just right. So, I tucked my skirt up into my apron and climbed up that tree. 'Hand me that saw,' I told him.

"He looked kinda shocked or scared or something, but he needed to get rid of that branch, so he handed me the saw. Well, I sawed and I sawed, and then when it was almost cut through, I pushed on it with my feet and it dropped right where I wanted it. It didn't hit the eave or nothin'!"

Rather than chastise her for performing dangerous tasks without an able adult nearby, Wallace made use of her shared story. "It wasn't one of your chores and you didn't get paid, but you helped someone because he needed it. Mr.

Flynn felt good about it, too. I remember seeing him later. Having that tree pruned so it didn't fall through his roof... Well, he couldn't have been happier if you bought him a new plow."

He paused, then amended his statement. "He couldn't have been happier if you'd bought him a new blade for his plow."

I put my crocheting back in the basket that Annie had made me, then took over the lesson.

"See, you gave a little of yourself and received a warm, wonderful feeling and so did Mr. Flynn. And you know what else? I'll bet the next time he sees you, he'll wave and say hi."

Jenny hunched forward and giggled into her hands. "He already did. And he said that next time we're coming near his place, he has a surprise for me. Well, I guess it isn't a surprise anymore, because when I asked him, he told me what it was. He gathered a whole bunch of seeds from his flower garden a couple months ago and he put aside some of them to share. He's going to give me a whole bunch of them. He said to make sure it was okay with you and Daddy before I start spreading them around, though. I mean, I don't think we want flowers growing in the corn field and between the tomatoes and squash, but maybe in between the peas would be okay, I mean, all right."

Before anyone could reply, we heard the footfalls on the porch.

"I thought James and family weren't coming over until tomorrow," Wallace said and stood to unlatch the door.

"Happy Christmas," Samuel said, and held up two dead wild turkeys by the feet.

"Samuel's here? Where's Annie? He brought Annie, too, right?" The children said one after the other.

Annie walked out from behind Samuel and handed Wallace a bundle. "For your next baby," she said.

I moved the children back so the couple could make it into the house. Suddenly, the baby started crying.

Scout walked up with wee Faith in his arms, wide awake, squalling like every other healthy, hungry baby. "I think the sound of excitement woke her. It's nearly time for her bottle, though." He looked up and smiled. "Why hello, Samuel. Greetings to you and your wife."

"Scout?" Samuel asked.

"Aye, 'tis me. I was wonderin' if they were speaking of ye

when tellin' the story of the tall man named Samuel who took their new friend Annie as a bride."

Annie totally ignored the men's chatter and quickly made her way to my elbow. I gently bounced the baby to keep her distracted while Jenny, the formula chef, was scalding the milk.

"Your baby?" Annie asked. "How? When?"

Tears were now spilling from her eyes. Here I had all these beautiful children and she had none. Whether or not she really couldn't have a baby was moot. Here I was with a new baby—obviously Indian, or at least half—and I hadn't even been pregnant.

"Here, do you want to hold her?" I said and stood up to offer her the chair.

Annie felt for the chair, but never took eyes off the baby as she sat down. "Yes. Please."

"She's a bit fussy, but we have a bottle coming for her." I looked at Scout to see if I could figure out what I should do or say, and then realized that Faith had stopped crying. Her eyes were wide open, her jaw slack as she looked at Annie with what could almost be called recognition.

"Ah, crap," I said, and turned away. "I'll be right back.

You have this, right?" I asked Jenny.

Jenny didn't know what to say or do about me but did know she needed to finish the bottle and formula for Faith. She nodded her reply, then bent back to her task, the uncertainty in her eyes nearly as loud as the fact that she hadn't responded with words. That girl was never mute!

No one had to tell me. I knew it in my bones. Faith needed to be with Samuel and Annie.

Wallace followed me out to the porch. "I'd ask you what's wrong," he said, and handed me a quilt for my shoulders, "But it's obvious."

"You saw it, too?"

"I know we'd be wonderful parents to Faith, but as an adult, or even a young child, she'd be ridiculed and scorned because she's different. We'd accept her, but society wouldn't."

"Yeah, well, that's one thing that really sucks about the 18th century—the prejudices. I hate to say it, but when I left in the early 21st century, it wasn't perfect, but no one batted an eye if a kid was a different ethnicity than the parents. Or not overtly. I mean, they didn't deny schooling or restaurant service or…"

I broke down sobbing.

"I just had a baby and now I'm going to lose her! You saw Annie. And if what she told us is true, then this is the only way she'll have a child, by adopting one."

Wallace re-wrapped the quilt around me, then chuckled.

"What's so cotton-picking funny?" I asked, glad that I had stopped the blaspheme before it came out.

"I guess Jenny was right again. Remember? She told Annie she'd have a baby. I guess this is the one, although…"

I could feel the shudder through Wallace's body. I realized what it was and shuddered right along with him. What a horrid way to get a baby. First the mother is murdered, then the brother—barely a teenager—had to cut it out of his dead stepmother to save it.

"Don't worry, Evie. We'll have more children. I may not have the sight like Jenny, but I know in my bones, we'll have more children."

"But…but…"

"But what? We were given the chance to save a woman from death, or worse, and now she has the opportunity to raise a child that probably wouldn't have made it into this world without the bravery of a very young man. Two lost lives found. They deserve each other. I don't know what Samuel's story is, but he seems a decent sort. And Scout knows him. If there was a character flaw, I'm sure I would have seen distrust or apprehension in Scout when they greeted. Don't worry, they'll be fine."

"Yeah, well it looks like Jenny's Christmas wish is coming true. She told me all she wanted was for Annie to be happy. Let's go in and make sure she is." I started to laugh and cry at the same time. "I don't think there's a reason in the world for Annie not to be happy when she finds out she just had a baby."

"Hmm," Wallace said, rubbing his chin. "I think we'll have to give them Sarah P as a gift. That nanny will have milk for at least a few more months, long enough until the baby is able to eat smashed people food."

10 Guilt

"I didn't think you'd mind if I let Annie feed Faith," Jenny said, her head tipped down slightly, indicating she felt a tinge of guilt.

I looked over at the new mother and daughter and couldn't help but be happy for them, the lone tear sneaking down my cheek one of joy, not sorrow, at the surprise addition to my family getting a new mother. I guess the tears of loss would come after Faith left with her new family.

"Pretty baby," Samuel said, stroking Faith's thick black hair. Milk pooled in her mouth as she looked up and smiled at him. Annie took the bottle away and wiped the overflow with the edge of the baby blanket.

"She needs a better home," I said softly, then put my hand on his arm. "An Indian home. I know you just got married, but could you and your wife handle a child, too?"

"My baby?" Annie asked, then clutched the baby closer, her eyes looking deep into mine, desperate to verify that she hadn't heard me wrong or that I was teasing.

I shrugged one shoulder and nodded. "If both you and your husband want her." I sniffed back another tear that had imposed on the conversation. "I guess Jenny was right about you having a baby. I just didn't think it would be so soon."

I wanted to turn away, run back to the porch—or further—wrap myself in my quilt and curl up in a corner, pretend this wasn't happening. But it was. No matter how I tried to justify keeping her, I always rebounded back to the fact that Faith belonged with this young couple.

"Ye don't have to keep her if she's a burden," Scout said. "By blood, she's my sister. I'd be proud if ye took on bein' her father, Samuel." He sighed and shook his head, thinking of his own—and Faith's—biological father. "Ye'd be a grand father. I dinna ken yer wife, but if ye chose her, I'm sure she'd be a fine mother, too."

"Easy choice," Samuel said, "even before you said she was your kin. Yes, we would be proud to be her new parents."

"Well, that's settled," Wallace said, his eyes red from the tears that were now on the back of his shirt sleeve. "I think we have a bit of time to spare before we have Jenny's *faux* ham for dinner. Who wants to help me pluck a couple of

Christmas turkeys?"

"I do! I do!" All three little ones chorused.

"I can help, too," Jenny said softly.

We could all tell that she said it out of obligation, not desire. It wasn't her normal tone and was sort of scary.

"Would you rather stay in here and tell Annie all about Faith? You know, her routine, how to calm her when she rouses in the middle of the night, the best way to burp her? You've been around her just as much as I have. I...um...want to help get those turkeys ready for tomorrow's dinner, too," I said.

It wasn't exactly the truth, but I had an armload of wishful thinking, hopes that my mind would be completely occupied somewhere else, even if it was with plucking pin feathers out of a turkey's butt. Besides, Wallace needed my help. Those were big birds. It was a tough job without wrangling our three competitive toddlers who were sure to make it a contest to see who could pluck the biggest feather.

***

"Are Annie and Samuel going to take Faith with them?" Wren asked.

"Yeah, huh?" echoed Judah.

I inhaled deeply, trying to find the right words, but was spared the chore by Wallace.

"Faith was living with us for just a little while, just like Annie was. They'll always be a part of our family. It's just that they won't be staying with us."

"Oh, all right," Wren said, then stood at my elbow, trying to decide whether she wanted to grab feathers or just watch.

"Yeah, that's all right," the boys said at the same time.

"She's cute, but kinda noisy," Judah said.

"Besides," Wren added, "We have River around if we want to play with a baby."

"Won't Grandpa and Granny be sad that they're gone when they come back?" Wren asked, her hands at her side, fumbling with her pockets rather than pitching in to pull out damp stinky feathers.

"Your Grandpa and Granny never met Faith, just Annie, remember? They've been gone so much this year. I was hoping they'd be back by Christmas, but since that's just a few hours away..."

I stopped talking and looked out the lone window in the barn at the starry sky. There was just a sliver of a moon. Clear and cold. No chance of a white Christmas this year.

Still, we had a warm house and our family kept getting bigger and bigger, even without me getting pregnant. I shook my head, dousing the sadness that was trying to sneak in by counting my blessings. I had so much. Every year, we had more and more as a family. And we were all healthy…

"Are you all right?" Wallace asked, his breath warm and welcome on my neck.

"Oh, I'm very all right. We may not have money, but we're about the richest people we know, save James and Leah maybe."

"Yes, our family as a whole has so much…"

Wallace didn't finish his remark, instead stayed still, listening. "Be quiet for a moment, children. I think someone's coming."

"Sandy Claws, Sandy Claws," Judah squealed.

His words were literally clamped off by Wren's hand over his mouth. "Daddy said to hush," she whispered, then took her hand off and wiped it on the skirt of her dress. "Ick," she said softly.

I looked to Wallace just as he faced me. "Company," we said.

"Stay here with your mother, children. Let me see who it

is and I'll be right back."

"Do you think it's Santa Claus?" Leo asked. "I said it right, huh?"

"Yes, you said it right, but I doubt it's Santa Claus. It might be your Grandpa Jody and Granny, though. Gee, I hope so…"

I really didn't know why I was hoping for more people in the house. I guess more distraction was good. Of course, I couldn't help but think of babies all the time now. It was my time of the month and I was hormonal enough without a major life change coming into the picture.

"It's Grandpa Julian!" exclaimed Wren. She beelined toward him for a tackle or hug or whatever it was. Julian could have stood his ground with just her coming at him, but he knew the other two were right behind her. He held onto the door frame and braced himself.

"Grandpa Julian, I'm glad you came! I'd rather have you than Santa Claus any day," Wren said, and hugged his leg even harder.

"My turn, my turn," the boys said, shoving each other out of the way for access to Julian's other side.

"Okay, children, let me get the horse inside. I have a few

items in the saddlebags. Maybe you can help me carry some parcels into the house." Julian looked up, saw me standing next to Wallace, and smiled.

"What are you two doing? Oh, it looks like someone got lucky and shot a turkey?" he stepped outside and led the horse in, the children guiding him as much as hindering him.

"Look again," I said when he returned. "There are two of them. Our friend Samuel gave them to us. And since when did you start saying 'okay'?"

"You and your mother are wearing off on me," he said with a sly smile.

Julian knew Sarah, Leah, James, and I were all from a future time, but we never spoke of it outright. Wallace and Jody knew, too, but only Julian treated it as a bit of forbidden knowledge, occasionally inferred, but never revealed.

"Then I guess you may have to wait to eat the ham I brought. I have a few other items that may interest you, too. How much more feather plucking do you have to do there, son?"

Wallace chuckled. "Almost done. I'd shake your hand, Papa, but I don't think you'd appreciate it. Boys, come over and help me finish this bird. The feathers are off, but someone has to pull out the innards."

"Me! Me! Me!" both boys chanted, jumping up and down in place.

"Not me," Wren said. "I'll take my turkey cooked, thank you very much."

"My, what lovely manners, Wren," Julian said. "I agree. Let the young men do the slippery work. Why don't you, your mother and I go in the house? You two can help me carry the parcels."

***

"Shhh," Jenny warned when we came in. "She just went to sleep."

Julian looked around and saw a couple he didn't know, a big Indian holding a very young baby in his arms and a beautiful woman at his side, leaning into him as only a happy wife would.

"Grandpa Julian!" Jenny exclaimed in a hoarse whisper. "I didn't see you coming!"

"Help me with these parcels, would you, dear, so I can give you a proper hug."

Jenny grabbed the ham out of his hand and set it in the middle of the table, then took the twined-tied bundles from

Wren and me and set them next to it.

"I made a ham, Grandpa Julian," she whispered. "It's not a real ham, but it looks like one. We're going to eat soon. Would you join us? Huh, please?"

"Come look," I said in a normal voice, and nodded for Julian to follow me. I lifted the lid off the Dutch oven and showed him the *faux* ham.

"You did this? All by yourself? And it's not meat?" Julian asked Jenny.

"Uh huh. Well, mostly not meat. It does have some bacon fat in it. Next time, maybe I can save some of the fat from your ham and cook it down 'til its runny and I can use that. This one tastes good, too, but it doesn't have a real bone, so it isn't good for soup or beans or nothin' like that. Hey! Where's Diego? He's not sick or nothin' is he?"

"Diego is fine. He's staying with the animals. One of these days, we may be able to hire some help, but for now, it's just us two old bachelors," he said and winked at me.

"You're not old and Diego is at least ten years younger than you," I said.

"Fifteen," he replied, "but who's counting."

Julian and Diego were partners in both life and the horse

breeding business. They were devoted to each other and really didn't care to be the fodder for rumors so had never hired help. Their lifestyle was their secret alone. The family held that secret even more sacred and hidden than our time traveling.

Stomp! Stomp! Stomp, stomp, stomp.

Two big men, two little men, and one average-sized woman came up the steps to the door. Jody let the little boys and Sarah come in first, reminding them with a whisper that there might be a baby asleep.

"Eek!" I squeaked, stifling the 'yahoo' that had been on its way out my mouth when I clamped my teeth together. "You made it!" I said and ran into Sarah for a full-bodied hug. "Oh, and you don't have to whisper, Jody. Faith is a sound sleeper. She'll wake when she's hungry. But please, no sudden noises, children."

"Just a moment," Wallace said, and brought his father forward. "I don't know if Evie made introductions yet, but Samuel and Annie, this is my father, Julian."

Samuel stood up and shook Julian's hand and nodded. *Another nice person had come into this house. No scowl or derision about his race in his features, and the man shook his hand and even smiled at his wife and child. Good people seemed to be attracted to this place.*

"Good to meet you and your family, Samuel," Julian said, then backed away so Jody and Sarah could meet the couple.

"And you already know my other father and mother, Jody and Sarah, but they haven't met your daughter, Faith."

Sarah immediately transitioned into doctor mode, threading her way between Leo, Judah, and Wren to see the very young baby. "But Annie, just a few weeks ago you weren't pregnant, were you? I mean, she looks just like you, but...but."

"She's their miracle baby," I said. "I'll explain later. Just know that mother, father, and baby are all fine. However, I think they're getting a gift we hadn't planned on giving. Sarah P will be going home with them."

Samuel looked at Wallace with a 'What's she talking about?' expression.

"We're giving you our nanny goat. You'll need milk for the baby."

Suddenly, Scout emerged from the corner, rubbing his eyes. "Sorry. I musta fallen asleep. Greetings Julian, Sarah, Jody. I'm glad ye made it in time for Christmas. Now, maybe it's the sleep still in my ears, but did ye say that yer givin' Sarah P to Samuel and Annie?"

"And Faith," Wallace said. "Is there a problem?"

Scout's mouth moved around as he thought, the words staying put until he had them sorted. "It's jest that Samuel only has the one mule. He could let Annie ride on it, then lead the mule and goat, but I think it might be better if I accompanied them. If somethin' happened, I'm sure he'd appreciate another set of hands."

Samuel swallowed hard. He wanted to believe that he alone could take care of his new family, and he knew he could if nothing unusual happened. But all it would take is for the goat to get loose and he'd be in a bind. He couldn't leave his wife and daughter alone while he chased the baby's food supply. He didn't have a goat or milk cow in his village or even nearby. He took a deep breath of gratitude. This young man would never insult him or try to make him feel inadequate. He was a gentleman, despite his youth.

"Yes, Scout, I would like it if you came with us."

"I heard about some of the hardships ye had. I'm fair at building structures, so I can help ye with that, too. And while yer tendin' to yer new wife and child, I'd be glad to help with anythin' else that needs done. I'm fair at trappin' rabbits, too."

"No polecats, please," Annie said and shook her head vigorously.

Almost all of us laughed. Julian, his face pinched in confusion, started to ask why she'd say that when Wallace said, "I'll explain later,"

"No. I dinna care to trap polecats," Scout said. "There are plenty of possums, squirrels, and rabbits and if I'm lucky, maybe a deer or elk. It's been a while since I lived in a village, and as much as I like bein' here, I'd rather be where I'm needed."

"But I need you, Scout!" Jenny said, then ran into his arms.

Scout patted her back, consoling her like the hurt child she was, at least emotionally. "I'll be back. I jest need to get Samuel and his family situated. Now, if ye were in the same place as Annie, wouldna ye want someone like me to come and help?"

Jenny sniffed a couple times while she thought, then finally admitted through broken sobs, "Yes. But come back in the summer. Or spring. Or maybe even next month…"

Scout shook his head at her. "I'll be back when it's time,"

he said, then wiped her tears with his shirt sleeve. "And I always ken where to find ye."

***

Leah, James, and their two youngsters came over after the introductions had been made. I guess Jenny was supposed to 'Morse Code' them when we were ready for them, but she forgot. Regardless, their timing was nearly perfect: Bibby Liz missed out on stringing popcorn and berries onto the string. I guess that was good, though, because at her age she'd rather eat the holiday decorations than make them. The Melbourne crew was in time for the stories and singing, though.

It was impossible to fit everyone at the table, even when we excluded the under thirteen crew, so Wallace brought in the milking stool and volunteered to eat with the children, balancing his plate on his knee. How I ever landed such a generous man, I'll never know…but I'll always be grateful for him.

Jenny's faux ham, turnips, and apples were a hit. With so many of us, we didn't have leftovers. The young boys actually took turns licking the platter clean. Well, they pre-cleaned it for me, anyway.

Bedtime came quickly, or so it seemed. Scout, Julian, and the young boys decided that they'd 'camp out' in the barn. Jenny and Wren took over the spot at the hearth, while Samuel, Annie, and the baby snuggled into the area Jenny and my youngest three usually slept in. No one slept in Jody and Sarah's bed while they were gone, no matter how crowded it got. That wasn't their rule, that was mine. Tonight, like always, it was clean and ready for them. When the yawns outnumbered the topics of conversation, James and Leah graciously backed out, promising to come over in the morning to help with Christmas breakfast.

***

"What are you doing in here so early?" I asked Julian as he tip-toed in the front door. "I don't even have the fire built up yet."

He brought out the parcel he had kept near him ever since he arrived. "I want to separate these gifts in the house," he whispered. "Go back to what you were doing. There's something in here for you, too."

"Hi, Grandpa Julian," Wren said, moving in under his arm to grab a hug. "I'm so glad you came. I'd rather see you than Santa Claus any day."

"Santa Claus? Did Santa Claus come?" Leo asked, Judah right behind him.

"Well, it looks like your sneaking out skills have faded, Julian," I said. "Boys, go back outside and use the privy."

"We already used the bush," Judah said. "It was closer."

The level of chaos and confusion rose from there for the rest of the morning, people of all sizes not yelling, but raising voices in order to be heard, folks practically stepping on each other. Actually, I think one of the boys did suffer a bruised hand from a boot at some point.

Annie had Jenny watch her make the baby's formula all by herself to make sure she didn't make a mistake. She said she did have a pan for boiling water at her new home, but not a ladle. I decided that it would be best if my spare one went with her family. It wasn't much of a gift, but sterilization was definitely a necessity for a month or two.

I fixed a big breakfast casserole with eggs, onion, and a bit of the ham Julian had given us. It was tight quarters again when James, Leah, and their two joined us for Christmas breakfast. Leah volunteered to cook one of the turkeys. They weren't as big as the commercial ones available in the 21ˢᵗ century, but were still decent sized. I didn't have room to cook two at the same time, but we definitely needed both of them for our big crowd. Jenny was put in charge of the 'smashed' potatoes, and James said he'd bring his dehydrated green beans and bell pepper dish. With the apple and pumpkin pies Leah and I had baked two days ago, we were set for our afternoon feast.

"Breakfast is finished, dinner menu and duties delegated, did we miss something?" Wallace asked with a big grin.

"Presents! Presents!" the little boys cheered. "Did Santa Claus come?"

"I'd still rather have Grandpa Julian," Wren said.

"Me, too," Jenny and Scout added.

"Well, I may not be Santa Claus," Julian said, "But I did bring a few gifts."

Julian doled out spinning tops to the boys and little hand mirrors to Jenny and Wren. Leah, Sarah, and I got a bag of buttons each.

"James, Jody, I hope you don't think I'm being rude or disrespectful, but I thought you'd know better what you'd like or need than I, so here." He handed them each a full silver Spanish dollar. "Buy what you need or want and consider it a gift from me and Diego. I couldn't ask for a better son and friend," he added, a hand on each man's shoulder.

"Thank you, Papa," Wallace said, and shocked his father by giving him a hug.

"Thank ye, Julian."

"I didn't know that you'd be here," he said to Scout, "but I've wanted to give this to someone special for a long time. You deserve it." Julian reached into his vest pocket and pulled out a ribboned medal. "It says 'for meritorious behaviour.' I think you deserve this. I've heard the tales of your brave deeds over the years. It's about time you got some recognition for it."

Scout wiped under his nose, his eyes sparkling with unshed tears. "A medal? For me? Thanks, Julian. This really means a lot to me." He held it up to the light coming in the window. "Is that a house or a shield? I canna tell."

"I believe it's a shield, as in you're a great defender, too," Julian said, adding a wink.

"My turn," Jody said. "We stopped in at Gibson's store on the way in. He said ye'd been in the store earlier, Wallace, but ye hadn't returned. He asked that we send this along fer yer wife."

Jody brought out a large folded piece of blue cotton calico. "I thought that maybe yer daughters would like some, too, so I bought a length of these fer both Jenny and Leah. Ye do like red and yellow, aye? Ye can decide amongst the two of ye which one."

The rest of the day just seemed to slip away. The boys played with their tops, Jenny showed Faith her image in the mirror, then Wren decided that she'd swap presents with Judah. Evidently, the top was more her style than seeing her reflection. I shared some of my fabric with Annie, and Julian gave Samuel part of the tobacco he had stashed in his saddlebag. The gift Annie brought for me was a soft woven blanket for the baby she knew I hoped for, not knowing about Faith. I asked her to give it to Faith instead. Her friendship and happiness was enough for me.

Dinner came together as planned, the turkeys finished roasting at the same time as the potatoes were done. James's contribution only took him a few minutes to rehydrate and warm, even without a microwave.

Full bellies, reflections on how blessed we all were, and pies finished off the perfect Christmas. Farewells were said, just in case someone overslept. Scout, Samuel, Annie and

Faith were going to be gone just before first light. Sarah suggested that Annie make three times the normal amount of formula and keep the extra in a glass jar tied close to her body. That would keep the formula at just the right temperature for Faith. She could add the formula to the baby bottle with ease as they were traveling. They'd have to skip sterilization for a couple of feedings, but that shouldn't be a problem.

There still wasn't any snow, but the air felt warmer. Hopefully, Samuel and company would make it to the village before snowfall.

Life was back to normal. Sort of. Something was still wrong with Jenny. I think it was because she missed Scout so much.

"Why don't you go visit James?" I said. "He always seems to make you feel better. Or at least he has enough projects you can help him with that you'll be distracted."

"Okay," she said glumly, her bottom lip pouched out so much, it looked like it had been stung by a bee.

***

"Hi," Jenny said to Leah, then gave Bibby Liz and River a hug. "Is James here?"

"You know he is. Go ahead and go out to the shop." Leah looked at her closer. "Are you all right? You don't look like yourself."

Jenny frowned. "Then who do I look like?" She snorted as she realized that Leah had made a joke. "Oh, I get it. I'm just sorta sad. I'll be fine. I wanna go see James. He always knows what to say when I'm blue. Or sad. Or bummed."

"There's my little helper," James said when she came into his shop. He saw her dour demeanor and jumped right into trying to bring her back to her bouncy, perky, full-of-optimism self. "Okay. Tell me what's wrong so I can fix it."

"I'm glad Annie's happy and that Faith now has parents who look like her and that Scout can help Samuel rebuild the village and help bring them fresh meat, but…but… I wanted him to stay here and live with us!"

James hugged her and said, "You and I both know he'll be back, right?"

Jenny looked up at James and squinted, trying to read his mind.

James saw and felt what she was doing, so quickly started thinking of the prime numbers in order. 1, 3, 5, 7, 11…

Jenny frowned at him. "I know what you're doing," she said with a scowl, then sighed and relaxed back into her brother-in-law's opened arm. "I may not know what you're thinking, but you're right. It'll all work out, huh?"

"Yeah, huh, Jenny" he said, almost calling her 'Granny' instead of Jenny.

13, 17, 19… He'd better concentrate on prime numbers before she found out the secret he'd been hiding since he time traveled here over a year ago, that she was his great-grandmother so many times over.

Jenny grinned. She didn't know what he was thinking—this time—but she knew it was warm and wonderful and she and Scout were part of it. Just like chasing Christmas, time had to pass until that day came. But it would. And then it would all come together and be perfect.

The End

THANK YOU!

Thanks for reading *Chasing Christmas*. If you'd like a chance at getting an ARC (advanced readers copy) of my upcoming books or find out random (and hopefully interesting) information, please sign up for Time Travelers Anonymous. I promise I won't plug up your inbox with loads of newsletters and I will not share your contact information with any other person or site. http://bit.ly/dhNewsltr

MORE stories with The Fairies Saga folks

If you'd like to find out more about the family in this story, there are lots of other books out there about the time traveling family and their friends Here they are in chronological order.

Naked in the Winter Wind (Lengthy novel) It all began with a tumble back in time where 'Evie' became involved with the fictional characters of a popular romance novel. A bottle of Fountain of Youth water, amnesia, abandonment, and adoptions complicated her new life in Revolutionary War era North Carolina. But the men were hot and the women tough. First appearance of Jenny and Scout in the series

Ha'Penny Jenny (Historical novella) A bit more about our young lady and her new family.

Aye, I am a Fairy: (lengthy novel) He's not what she thinks he is, but he can help her in her time travel dilemma. Lots about James and Leah, Scout and Jenny in this one.

Dances Naked: (novel) Directionally challenged British lord is trying to get back to his family in the 21st century when he is found by a Cherokee hunting party. What will it take to get the chief to lead him to the Trees, the portal through time?

Little Bear and the Ladies (Historical novella) The gentle 18th century trapper we first met in NITWW steps in to save the day for the survivors. Now what's he going to do with so many women?

The Great Big Fairy: (lengthy novel) Benji finally returns to his grandparents in the 18th century, but he didn't plan on acquiring a very strong, and stubborn, female slave who can't—or won't—speak.

Little Drummer Boy (Historical novella) Young Scout wants to earn money as a scout but is told he's only good enough to be a drummer boy. Can he help the others find their way during one of the worst snowstorms of the 18th century?

Never Too Young (Historical novella) Scout is older now, and managed to earn enough to return to Jenny and provide her with a proper home, but will a con artist ruin his plans? And after the long separation, will she still be waiting for him?

Pool Boy Wanted: No Experience Preferred (a rather racy novella) He'd do anything to save his friend, and she knew it. Bad cougar! Find out about Benji's reference to his bad experience with a woman from Luke the Unexpected here.

Luke the Unexpected: (novella) How can he get the attention of the hot blonde who loves motorcycles as much as he does? A bit of Benji here in this story

Time in a Little Blue Bottle (time travel 'mash up' novella) Elvis, Mark Twain, and the prime vampire are racing to get the bottle of Fountain of Youth water before sweet Bella and the youthful pickpocket. So why are time travelers Marty Melbourne and Master Simon interested?

Other books by Dani Haviland

Kit Kringle: An Alaskan Tale (contemporary novella) Falling in love was not part of her business plan.

Be My Angel: Wyatt's dream to help save the wild mustangs began with the purchase of a rundown ranch in western Oregon. What he hadn't anticipated was being mesmerized by a sassy woman in a wheelchair.

A Stingray Christmas (romantic suspense) The first book in the Arlie Undercover series finds our Alaska detective on his way to Arizona to recover and discover.

The Biggest Heart Ever: (Book two in the Arlie Undercover series) When would Arlie learn that trying to do everything by himself could be deadly—and make Charlene a widow before they were married?

Always a Bigger Fish: (Book three in the Arlie Undercover series) Back in Alaska, Arlie finds out he's a target. Will vacationing detective Billy Burke (from THE FAIRIES SAGA) have information to help nab the scalper?

CONTACT INFO:

http://bit.ly/DaniHaviland

https://www.facebook.com/dani.haviland

Amazon Author page http://bit.ly/2authorDH

Twitter @dani_haviland

Book Bub Author page http://bit.ly/BBDani

Goodreads http://bit.ly/2DHgdrds

Blog: http://bit.ly/DHbLog

Email: dani@danihaviland.com